CW01018462

For June.
best wishes.

OUT OF THE BLUE

Pauline Slater-Etheridge

P. S. Etheridge.

© Pauline Slater-Etheridge 2007

ISBN 978-0-9556553-0-2

All rights reserved.
Without limiting the rights under copyright
reserved above, no part of this publication may be
reproduced, stored in or introduced into a retrieval system,
or transmitted, in any form or by any means
(electronic, mechanical, photocopying, recording
or otherwise) without the prior written permission of
both the copyright owner and the publisher of this book.

Printed by
The Amadeus Press, Cleckheaton, BD19 4TQ

This is the first Novel
by Pauline Slater-Etheridge.

For the last twenty five years of her working life the Author worked as a Local Government officer, firstly in the Borough Treasurer's department in the local Town Hall but mainly in the Housing department of that same authority.

She has always had the urge to write and has had several short stories and articles published over the last years.

Retired and in the Autumn of her own years she has fulfilled her ambition to write a novel and feels that the experience has been extremely fulfilling.

She feels that if you read the book, you will grow to love Joe as much as she does.

She is now widowed but has a married daughter and three grandchildren.

ACKNOWLEDGEMENTS

I am greatly indebted to Joel Breeze for his illustration on the cover of the book.

Also, to Mr. Ernest Ormerod for his helpful comments and facts about life in the National Service in the 1950s, who together with my late husband Tony, provided me with great insight into their experiences.

To my dear friends Dorothy and Mollie High for their proof reading, my sister Valerie and other great friends who have all been very supportive in urging me to pursue and fulfil the dream.

Thank you all.

SYNOPSIS

"OUT OF THE BLUE"

This is a bitter sweet story mainly about one man. His name is Joe John Bullimore and he has almost reached retirement age. Unfortunately, he has recently become redundant and is quite downhearted.

As he reminisces nostalgically, and in great depth about his past life, which initially started in a small mill town in Yorkshire, he remembers in detail the happy events, the traumas and the tragedies of his life up to now, and leaves him wondering what the future holds.

Fortunately, fate takes a hand and the circumstances surrounding him at the present time offer him more than an element of hope.

Pauline Slater-Etheridge.

Chapter One

Joe had almost finished shaving when he nicked his chin with the razor. He frowned as he dabbed it with a tissue and pencilled in some antiseptic stick. He quickly rinsed his face, towelled it dry, splashed on some after shave lotion wincing as it initially stung his cheeks, noticing the redness of his face in the mirror from the vigorous rubbing.

That was not all that he noticed as he quickly glanced back again at his reflection. Whose face was it? Whose sad and doleful eyes? The man in the mirror did not look like him at all. Alright, he was older and he did not like it, but it was a fact, and it was acceptable. This man though was so different to the man that he had been perusing in the same way some three months ago.

He stood back, away from the mirror to assess himself. Yes, they were his eyes, still blue and clear, no signs of cataracts or other deformity, but they were dead eyes, absolutely lifeless.

He crinkled up his face into some kind of smile, which was more of a grimace, but it was false, not spontaneous and the eyes remained as before, unsmiling. It scared him. He could not control it. He had never been what anyone would call exceptionally good looking, but his face, he thought had been pleasant enough and had always shown a trace of character but now, well?

The hair he considered was still quite thick. White, but

thick and he supposed modestly that perhaps that was worth something.

After quickly showering and dressing he made his way downstairs. Breakfast was always on the table. That could always be guaranteed and so he sat down, crossed his legs and proceeded to pour out the coffee and butter the toast before it went totally cold. He would not object, he never did, but he did breakfast alone as usual.

He glanced out of the window and it was a nice pleasant day. Trudie would be in the garden, pruning and weeding but more than likely she would be keeping a lookout as usual.

He scolded himself for his bad thoughts but there had been so many examples in the past that he could not think of anything otherwise at all.

He contemplated clearing away the breakfast things from the table, but then hesitated, and decided not to bother because he feared that he would not do it correctly if he did. Then again if he didn't he would most probably be in trouble anyway, so he decided to leave them and craned himself wearily out of the chair. For Trudie, there was always a place for everything and everything in its place. Best leave it.

He continued on into the hallway and through the front door. He called out into the garden to tell his her that he was going out, asking at the same time if she needed anything bringing back.

A slim, wiry woman raised her head and scowled ferociously and without answering his question she snapped "You do raise yourself sometime don't you? Now you are going out again. You never stay in".

It was only eight thirty a.m. How early was he supposed to get up? After all, he had no work to go to, not any more. He sighed yet again. He must not succumb to that awful depression again today. He was determined not to allow her to drive him into a black mood again. She seemed to enjoy seeing him look saddened and miserable. She was right though, he never did look anything else but miserable, but whose fault was that?

He walked over to where she was pruning off some dead bush heads and fell short of continuing what he had to say, when she was distracted somewhat by the arrival of a gleaming red car pulling in and braking to a halt at a neighbour's house. The car door opened to reveal a lovely looking young woman. She alighted from the vehicle, with a distinctive air of class. She was beautifully dressed and smiled pleasantly at them both before politely saying "Good morning". Joe reciprocated with the same, "Good morning". Trudie declined rudely and the young woman continued to walk up the path and into the neighbour's house.

Trudie turned now to face Joe. "I might have known that you would speak to her," she snapped once again. "You could never resist talking to women and I bet that one has never done one days work in her life! All got up like a dog's dinner," she snarled, but in the next breath continued. "I do wonder though, why she should be visiting Barbara Hall? Probably a niece." She finished her tirade, miffed at not knowing more about the visit but clearly intending to carry on scouting.

Joe completely ignored her latter comment with the disgust it deserved and continued on to explain why he had responded to the young woman's politeness. "I will speak to anyone and you know that. It is only courteous to acknowledge people and especially when they speak to you first. Anyhow, I will not discuss such infantile topics with you and I will not argue with you. I am sick to death of arguing with you. You are an evil, awful woman and I have had enough. I said that I was going out. I don't know when I will be back. You will see me, as they say, when you see me."

With that Joe stormed off. He did not look back. Trudie would no doubt be astonished at his outburst because it was not like him to fly off the handle like that. He usually took everything quietly as he had always felt that it was easier that way, but now he felt that he could not curb his self-control any longer. All the nasty back-biting, the complaining, the snide remarks and not just in the recent weeks but all his married life. It had been somewhat easier when he had worked, he could get away from her and enjoy a laugh and good conversation with colleagues and friends, but ever since his redundancy he had no such outlets and therefore, no real future that he could foresee. These thoughts, and the desolation appertaining to these thoughts, clouded him with depression. He would have to do something, but what?

He was so upset that in his mind it was very hard to think straight. He was tired and weary of thinking at all.

All his married life he had been miserable. He had no one to blame but himself. He was too soft natured which could be more of a vice than a virtue, and had certainly not done him any good at all. He had never shown any assertiveness, only tolerance. He had been too busy, for too long thinking that things would turn out to be better if he persevered. When his son David had come along, well, he had to be well and truly planted in the homestead, because he would never have left him.

As he walked along his mind was coasting in all directions, hopping around like a grasshopper from one marital disaster to another. There had been a time when he had suggested, not insisted, they had a divorce, years ago. The hassle evolving from the suggestion had been staggering. Threats, tears, tantrums, promises, all amounting to Joe feeling sorry for upsetting her, and reproaching himself for his naivety and for being so insensitive, after all, their problems could have been his fault too.

He knew now with hindsight that he had not really been at fault at all. That he had been stupid to fall for her theatricals. Since that time, Joe had thought long and hard about moving out. Even if it had meant that he did not bother to obtain a divorce from her. Just to get away would have been enough. The idea had started to form in his imagination. He would leave soon and buy a small flat. Something modest. Nothing fancy, just somewhere far enough away for her not to keep on pestering him. He could buy basic furniture and add to, as and when he went along. The more he had thought about it the more appealing and exciting the thought was. The plan began to materialise positively and steadily in his mind until that awful day when any idea of such an immediate escape crumbled cruelly away.

....

Many years ago he had moved his family from Yorkshire to Nottingham because of a job promotion. Being an accountant he had many job offers and career moves, but this one was different because there had been the promise of a possible partnership. Unfortunately, after the premature death of the owner the partnership had never materialised and being Joe he never pressed or tried any real alternatives. He had never had sufficient ambition to start up a business of his own although, it was never for the want of qualifications, and it would have been financially viable, but he had preferred to carry on in the same vein, in the sincere hope that another alternative might arise. That is, until three years ago when he was flattered to be head hunted by an extremely reputable firm back here in his beloved Yorkshire. He did not hesitate to take the job, they were not offering a partnership at this time, but by now Joe had ceased to have any illusions or ambitions at all about his future. He was content to work for an employer and not to have to deal with the responsibility of being a boss. He thought that Trudie might at least be happier nearer her relations and friends, few though they were, back in Yorkshire, but of course, true to form she was not. He was though. He had settled in nicely and had enjoyed every moment since, that is, until five months ago, when the firm declared that they were ceasing business and that the staff had all of one week to find elsewhere to work. Of course redundancies would be paid, but the shock of it all was terrific for all concerned. Joe had not worked there for very long, and what chance of further employment was there going to be for him at his age? He was sixty three years of age and he felt that he could not face a life with only Trudie, and depression set straight in. He could not at that moment think of another alternative or another way out at all.

....

Quite suddenly, Joe became aware of a wet sensation at the back of his hand. He realised that he must have been sitting on this bench in the park for quite some time. A friendly little dog had raced up and greeted him with a kiss on his hand. He smiled at the little creature, who in turn appeared to be laughing at him, its eyes aglow and with its tongue hanging out with breathlessness, eagerness and hopeful anticipation of an equally happy reception it might get from Joe, which the little mite did. Joe had always loved animals of any kind, pedigree or cur, wild or domesticated. He gazed with pleasure at the animal and stroked it until eventually its owner called it back and it sped obediently away.

He had never been allowed any pets. 'Too dirty in the house', he remembered Trudie stating with some disdain. The thought made him angry with himself. What kind of man was he? Could not have a dog, indeed! Why had he not insisted? Time to change he thought adamantly. Time to change and now!

Joe settled back on the bench now feeling more comfortable and relaxed. The sun was shining and the trees and the flowers were all in full bloom. What could be nicer he thought, but his weary mind still drifted off again. He was comfortable with his thoughts. His thoughts were all he had.

…………………….......

"Are you a funny fella?"

Joe came to and saw a young boy around eight years old. "A funny fella?" Joe repeated back to him. "What do you mean?"

"My Mum says I haven't to talk to strangers 'cos they might take me away". The boy stood back now ready to fly away at the first sign of Joe making any movement which might be interpreted as dangerous.

"No, I am not a funny fella I can assure you but IF I were I would not be telling you that, now would I? The best advice that I can give you is not to talk to anyone unless your mother is with you, because it could be very dangerous for you."

The boy bristled now and stuck out his tongue, his face

grimacing menacingly, he obviously did not like being scolded, even if it was a gentle telling off for his own sake.

"Anyway" continued Joe, ignoring the child's embarrassed rudeness, "shouldn't you be in school? Does your mother know that you are out here in the park on your own?"

"Course she knows where I am, I asked her first if I could come, and I'm not at school 'cos I've got chicken pox".

Joe raised his eyebrows. "Are you sure? I can't see any spots".

The child placed his hands on his hips in an exasperated manner and sighed at Joe's obvious ignorance. "That's all you know. My spots are under my T-shirt and on my bottom parts".

Again Joe smiled at the boy, he crinkled up his nose and feigned an itch. "Gosh! I bet they tickle".

"No they don't, my mum puts Calomine lotion on them, and anyway you can't catch 'em now 'cos I'm out of the inoculation period".

Joe smiled, again more broadly now at the wrong word used by the youngster. He was obviously trying to quote his mother. "I think you mean the incubation period, but no matter, you have the right idea and thank you for telling me because I do not think I would have known that", he said humouring the boy.

The child seemed pleased at the praise and smiled back shuffling on his feet. "I'm going now", he said, and with that turned to run off and was gone as quickly as he had come.

Joe watched the boy until he disappeared out of sight and smiled at his appearance. T-shirt, shorts, baseball cap, placed the wrong way around, and trainer shoes which made his feet look twice their size. How times had changed. Our children look more like American kids every day, but still, he realised it was much better and more casual than the attire his generation wore in his day.

Chapter Two
REMINISCENCES

Joe must have dropped off to sleep because he awoke with a start. He glanced at his watch and it was two o'clock. "My God!" he thought gasping in disbelief, fully hoping that no one would have noticed as they passed by. He was so embarrassed but had to admit that he still felt extremely comfortable and at ease sitting there and had to face the fact that there was absolutely nothing at all to rush about for. He had plenty of time to waste. Nothing especially he wanted to do at all.

He started to reflect affectionately on his conversation with the small boy. At least he had made him smile again. Surely that was something. All may not be lost.

He began recapitulating over his own childhood and remembered that it had been a very happy one, even though much of the time the war was in full force it was a much safer one by far for children playing out. No one really knew of any 'funny fellas' then he mused.

He drifted off into nostalgic bliss. He had been born into, what some might say at that time, a 'bit better off' family. His father Bob had a nice secure job working for the Local Council in the Town Hall Borough Treasurer's department, and his mother, Celia, was a part time midwife and health visitor.

Their house was a modest semi detached house with just two bedrooms and average sized gardens back and front. They had a garage and a greenhouse. His father grew tomatoes, gherkins, onions, cucumbers and such. The only flowers he grew were chrysanthemums, which he showed every year and received prizes for. He could not grow any other flowers in the garden because of the war as everyone with even a tiny bit of land had to utilise it in a proper manner and grow vegetables. He grew almost everything – potatoes, peas, beans, cauliflowers, red and green peppers and cabbages. He always had quite a surplus of all the produce which he sold without any problem to people who were not fortunate enough to have their own garden, or allotments which were rented if they were lucky enough to obtain one from the local council.

His mother used to make jam and preserves from the apples, plums and raspberries and pickle the gherkins, onions, beetroot, and red cabbage. Some of them she kept in her larder to last all year round and the rest she gave away as presents.

His father had been unable to fight in the war because of some minor heart defect, but he was a fire-watcher and worked regular night shifts on a rotation basis with other men. Joe remembered how he had sometimes arrived home late at night, but now and then he would be on an earlier shift thus allowing Joe to come downstairs occasionally for a treat, to sip a beaker of cocoa with them, and have some truffles, which his mother had made from dried milk, and condensed milk, all rolled into little balls and coated with cocoa and sugar. He would listen intently to what was going on in the neighbourhood and sometimes he was allowed to listen to either Paul Temple detective series, or ITMA with Tommy Handley, or even Valentine Dyall, who was the mysterious 'Man in Black'. All on the precious radio, which was everyone's lifeline to world events in those days.

He remembered fondly how his father had laughed heartily at the antics of the ITMA team and his mother had wished that she had had a voice as sexily husky as Steve, who was Paul Temple's wife and detective sidekick.

To live in a semi detached house in a textile town in those days gave some kind of status, although at that time Joe could never understand why. The majority of his friends all lived in rows of terraced houses. He played out with them constantly and even though they held him in some kind of esteem he never took advantage and could accept that they had thought that he was 'better off'. Now with hindsight he knew that he must have been.

Most of the men in the country were away fighting abroad, the rest were either working in the munition factories, making arms for the fighting men, in the textile mills or down in the coal pits, mining. The women were allowed to stay at home if they had dependant children or were ill, but the rest of them worked with the men or had alternatively enlisted in the armed forces to help the war effort. His mother had continued with her nursing profession. Most of the women were very industrious, either knitting for the armed forces or crocheting blankets, but the most significant thing he could remember about those days was the wonderful state of morale. Camaraderie, uniting everyone. Friendships were founded and real community spirit formed. It was strangely a spectacular time to live in.

Every one of the children became friends and every street appeared to have a 'gang' all their own, with only friendly rivalry between them. Everybody enjoying frivolous fun and games and most children oblivious of the terrible traumas of the time.

Keith Sutton though was his best friend. They went absolutely everywhere together, practically joined at the hip. Every season of the year was great, even the winter. So much to do. So many things, never a moment of boredom. The summers seemed to be long and warm, even though he now realised that there must have been bad weather some of the time, but those times were never memorised.

He remembered happily about the times when their 'gang' would go off to the local ruins and wade about in the beck, taking with them pop bottles full of water. The bottles had all to be returned to the shop to be refunded for the precious pennies or 'coppers' as they were known as then. They had also taken jam sandwiches, home made bread wedges wrapped hygienically in clean greaseproof paper. The wrapping had also to be taken back home to deter them all from littering and encouraging recycling. Everything had to be utilised but it was never a problem, it became a habit to save and was made into a real adventure.

Every season, there was a game to play in unison with all the other children. Whips and tops, skipping, marbles and hopscotch, when all the mothers would come out shouting about the chalk marks on the clean causeways, which they had scrubbed meticulously every week together with their outside steps, and they took great pride in competing with their neighbour.

Football was not seasonal, it was played all the time, along with cricket and rounders and even the girls could partake of the sports providing they promised to keep their eyes on the games and not try to kiss the boys, because that was sissy stuff, and any boy seen to encourage it would be marked a 'pansy' for life. He recalled that some of the girls were 'proper daft' playing silly games like 'one potato, two potato, three potato, four', a rhyme that seemed to go on forever and never getting anywhere. The boys used to scoff and girls like those were strictly taboo unless they could redeem themselves by listening to 'Dick Barton', special agent or 'Biggles' the ace pilot, on the wireless, and only if they could prove that they could remember the storyline, otherwise they were not to be believed.

The churches and chapels played a great part in everyone's lives. Sundays were for praying but during the week there was always something happening like socials, beetle and whist drives, sales of work and concerts. These were the places where the women would get together and discuss everything, from how the war was progressing to who was "expecting" or "due". Conversations always whispered so that the children did not hear, but they inevitably did and would go away and giggle about it. The word 'pregnant' was never mentioned because that was supposed to be indelicate.

He sat there and sighed. How things have changed.

Joe remembered how he had felt very grateful for their indoor toilet and bathroom He did not envy his pals who had to go outside and sit in a draughty 'midden' which had to have some kind of paraffin lamp installed in the wintertime to stop the cistern from freezing up. He smiled as he recalled the lack of toilet paper, and grinned widely as he remembered how the newspapers had been cut neatly into squares, threaded with string and hung on nails at the back of the lavatory doors, and if you were really lucky you could save any tissue papers from around the oranges, that is if you could get the oranges in the first place. Alternatively, he shuddered at the thought of the galvanised baths that were used by most folks, usually every Friday, filled from the pot boiler which was fired from the fire on the hearth and the first one to bathe was the youngest, the last one was usually poor mum or dad.

Nevertheless, even that was an event and usually taken in front of a lovely roaring fire, providing you could obtain the coal, then it was saved up during the week as a special treat. Friday night was bath night, when hair would be washed and soaped with 'Derbac' soap to keep the child free from head lice and nits. The rest of the week the children were stuck into the sink and 'top and tailed'. Every night of the week you were given a dose of cod liver oil and malt just to keep your stamina up and give you the vitamins they thought you might be lacking with your limited diet, in the hope that you could avoid illnesses. All the children were given milk at school for the same reason. Nevertheless, it did not stop everyone from getting the usual children's ailments, and some would be stricken down with scarlet fever or diphtheria, and sometimes infantile paralysis, now known as 'poliomyelitis', and they had to be incarcerated in isolation hospitals for quite a long duration of time and the child could not be discharged and sent home until that patient had been 'fumigated', usually in a bath of liquid tar in order not to infect anyone else. Even he and almost every child he knew, had their tonsils and adenoids surgically extracted. It appeared to be the norm in those days. "Got a sore throat? Whip 'em out!"

....

The war came to an end in Germany and Japan the same year as Joe passed his eleven plus examination to go to the grammar school. His parents had naturally been proud as punch, and his mother had gone out immediately to buy him his new school uniform. He remembered standing in the front of her wardrobe mirror examining his appearance. Sparkling new from top to toe. Shiny black shoes, grey knee socks with a blue stripe around the tops, short grey trousers, pure white shirt, black school tie with a blue stripe and a blazer in black, with the same colour braid piped around the edges. His school cap, placed snugly on his head, boldly sporting a badge with the school emblem. He had felt good as he put his new starkly stiff satchel across his shoulder and was rather proud of himself, but still he was very apprehensive about starting the new school. He knew that previously he had been one of the smarter children at the junior school but now he appreciated that he would be in competition with other boys who would all be equally as clever, and was a little dubious about being able to compete on a reasonable level.

"No matter, I will do what dad says and try my best and that is all that I can do", he had thought.

After that he had lost touch with a lot of his old chums, simply because he had always seemed to be busy doing homework. By the time he had finished it, and piano lessons, it had been too late to go out. He still went quite regularly to the local youth clubs with Keith, who was still his best pal and soul mate. They went to school together and collaborated on homework all the time. 'Both for one and one for both', was their undying motto.

Joe discovered that he was able to compete with the other pupils in all the lessons but that English Literature, English Language and Mathematics were the subjects that he excelled in.

He became a devout rugby player and enthusiast and went swimming as often as he could until eventually, his mother commented jokingly, that he was never to be reminded these days to wash behind his ears and the back of his neck. Joe had not realised, and became embarrassed by the fact that she had even noticed. He did not thank her for mentioning it. She was right though. He did take more notice of his appearance. He liked to keep his hair tidy, his trousers creased and his shoes polished. Could this be what adults called 'growing up'?

He soon realised that it was. After that, growing up crept up fast. The girls looked different and wow! Some of them even looked nice. The 'Dandy' and the 'Beano' comic days were over. Look out world the long trouser brigade are here, and here we come!

The days of going out with his parents to the local Empire Theatre to watch "The Saxon Players", who were in the repertory company and the variety shows, were over. Carol Levis could keep his discoveries and even if Julie Andrews did make an appearance with her parents, Ted and Barbara, he was not bothered any more. Keith and himself had discoveries of their own to make. The world was now their oyster and they had better make the most of it before they were called up into the armed forces to complete their National Service.

Whilst they were still at college neither he nor Keith could afford cars. Not many people could, but they were indulged by their respective parents, who all contributed generously towards their Lambretta scooters for eighteenth birthday presents. Together, they sped off from town to town, crash helmets donned, looking more like 'flyers' headgear than anything, and college scarves flying precariously in the wind. My, did they think they were quite something!

Every town had its own dance halls. This was the era of the BIG bands, all with a special sound all their own. The Glen Miller sound was still being imitated and played by some bands in honour of the great man who was so tragically lost in the war. Other bands preferred to have their own unique sounds. Joe Loss, Ted Heath, with vocalists like Lita Rosa, Dickie Valentine and Denis Lotis, the latter two becoming heart throbs to the girls, singing their ballads and swinging music. Frankie Laine giving out renditions of 'Jezebel' and Guy Mitchell with 'She wears Red Feathers and a Hoolie Skirt' and 'Chic a boom, Chic a rac'. Jazz clubs were frequented during the week when studies allowed and late night swing sessions at weekends, were an exciting outlet, when Joe would participate on the piano as often as he was allowed by the musicians concerned. Experiments with booze and smoking became the norm but drugs were never but never entertained. Strictly taboo.

There were dances in the wintertime almost every Friday night after college was finished for the evening.

Anything from Fireman's, Police, College, Valentine's to Saint Patrick's and everyone seemed to go. The girls in full dirndl skirts, with tulle net layers underneath to make them stand out. A lot of the young men in Edwardian style clothes, 'Teddy Boy' outfits as they were known, some much more extreme than others who faded into oblivion in comparison. Joe and Keith did adventure a little and indulged in 'D.A.' haircuts, first modelled by the film star Tony Curtis in his heyday, but were considered by some lads to be somewhat straight and conservative, but neither of them ever bothered about what others thought of them, they could pull the best girls, you know the more intellectual types hm.

Then Joe remembered that he had started to fancy himself in politics. He had no ambitions or aspirations to be a politician as such but he did enjoy debates and participation. He became a party member, and enjoyed making his points of view and opinions known and so he had promptly joined the Conservative party.

His grandfather had been a local Business man, and Liberal Mayor of the town, and Joe was always quite proud of the fact that his roots held some little importance in local history during the early days of the textile industry.

Eventually, when members of the Young Conservatives Association were travelling to the Isle of Man for their convention, Keith and himself had been included in the entourage. The debates and speeches had been stimulating during the daytime proceedings, but the nights had been equally exciting, and had resulted in him falling head over heels in love for the very first time and he didn't know what had hit him.

The convention was held in the local Villa Marina dance hall and afterwards at the end of the week they had held a dance.

Ronnie Aldrich and the Squadronaires were playing, when he noticed this divine looking girl, the epitome of grace and sophistication, standing near a column and smoking a luxurious cigarette which she had just taken from a swanky looking flat red box with gold lettering on it, and swaying to the vigorous strains of "Dragnet". She was wearing an off the shoulder dress in turquoise brocade and her hair cascaded and fell almost to her waist in golden blonde tresses. She had a pert little nose and a full luscious mouth that needed kissing.

His heart tumbled over and took his breath away. They did not make girls like this at home and he soon whisked her off onto the ballroom floor. He did not let her go for the rest of the evening, which clearly flattered her, and equally appeared to amuse her. Poor Keith. He had had to be satisfied with her girlfriend, which turned out to be a real turn of events as usually it was Joe, who was palmed off with the girlfriend. The goddess's name was Regina, "Gina" and she was really quite something.

His new amour came from the Midlands but she had no sign at all of an accent. She went to Oxford University and planned to become a doctor, in order to go to a foreign land, yet to be decided upon, and had very good intentions.

After the convention they all kept in touch by letter and eventually all four of them went camping in Provence, France, for the summer holidays. They had a great time, in spite of the fact that there was still much evidence around of the Nazi invasion during the war, but the local people were friendly, still remembering with gratitude what they owed the British people and so they were all welcomed with open arms, even though the locals were still struggling to recover from the many years of hardship.

Joe lost his virginity on that holiday and gained immeasurable experience in sex. As far as he was concerned this was the romance of a lifetime, but Gina had other ideas, and it was not too long after that holiday that she wrote to say, "Sorry", but she did not want any serious commitments at this stage in her studies but could they still be friends? Joe was devastated but was surprised to find how quickly he got over it. Life was too short for remorse. There were other fish to fry and so he got on with it.

Chapter Three

Sitting outside his father's garden hut, Joe remembered fondly of listening to the deep baritone voice of Edmund Hockeridge, throatily giving out a sweet rendition of 'Hey there! You with the stars in your eyes'. His mother came outside to hand him a envelope which had just arrived. Her eyes were a bit moist and her expression very doleful and he knew immediately that 'it' had come at last and he ripped open the envelope in anticipation and some trepidation. O.H.M.S., Would Mr. Joe John Bullimore be sure to attend for an interview and medical assessment at Templar House, Lady Pitt Lane, in Leeds on Tuesday of the next week, promptly, at fourteen hundred hours. He promptly went like a dutiful son of his country and another phase of his life was about to begin.

……………………........

Joe had sat quietly in the reception area of that building for about half an hour. It had amused him by reminding him of a doctor's surgery where everyone turn their heads automatically to see who is coming through the door but no one speaks once they are in. Some of the young men were looking totally relaxed, and others were shuffling about in their seats and lighting cigarettes to calm their ragged nerves. Everyone's body language said it all. Everyone could be read. How was he being read, he wondered? Actually, to be truthful, apprehensive as he was, he was quite looking forward to the adventure.

"This way", shouted a gruff voice, three stripes showing the speaker to be a sergeant and pointing to Joe. In Joe went like a lamb to the slaughter, suddenly feeling much less confident. His legs weakened somewhat as he sat across the desk from his interviewer.

The sergeant shuffled his papers and started to ask what type of service Joe preferred to enlist into.

"I am not exactly sure, I would like to discuss what options are open to me", Joe almost stammered and wondering how his confidence could have evaporated so quickly.

"Well. The Army, The Navy or the Air Force?" the man said loudly and abruptly.

"I never did like to sail particularly. It makes me quite sick". Joe said lamely.

The sergeant raised his eyebrows, mockingly, Joe thought.

"I am a bit scared of flying, although I have flown on holidays, but I would not make a habit of it unless I was forced". Joe knew that he was waffling and the sergeant was looking at him in disbelief.

"Well lad, that only leaves the Army and I do not suppose you have the stamina to be a marine, do you?" he continued, rather too sarcastically.

"I don't mind being in the Army". Joe began to prickle, thinking that this man should appreciate that these young men had never been in this position before. He felt that they should be given encouragement and not ridiculed by either word of mouth or looks, and then he realised that this kind of conversation was said to be the general carry on in the armed forces. No mollycoddling here!

Joe continued, "A lot of my friends are enlisting in the

Army".

"Any particular regiment?" The sergeant sighed as though he had asked these questions many times before and was totally miffed.

"Some of my pals are going into the Kings Own Light Infantry and I wouldn't mind being in the same regiment as them". Joe had said quickly not wanting to take up much more of the sergeant's time and also wanting to shorten the interview as much as possible.

"The K.O.Y.L.I. regiment eh? Well they are a good lot but you cannot really learn a trade, you know. Do you think that shooting and walking is going to be enough for you? You are a college lad and I thought you might like something a bit more ambitious".

"Not really", Joe answered. "I am not anticipating making a career of it after my National Service".

"Fair enough then. Go through that door into the next office and give the staff these papers and everything will be fixed. You will be notified shortly about the date and the destination of your camp. Thank you", he said stiffly, and with that he motioned for Joe to go and then stood up ready to walk over to the door for the next victim on the list.

It was eight weeks before he received any further contact from that department, but they only gave him one week's notice to be ready and present at Strensall Barracks in Yorkshire.

His father had driven him in his car to the station. His mother had been banned. He could not have coped with the embarrassment of his mother trying to control her emotions and he being humiliated in front of some of the lads he knew, who were all setting of at the same time as he was from the station. "Trouble is", he told himself, "I should not be an only child. If I had siblings she would

28

have other children to take her mind off my going away".

"It will only be a month mum, before you see me again", he had told her, but she would not be pacified.

…………………….........

The camp had looked stark, but tidier than anything he had ever seen. The corporal on duty looked severe. Joe smiled at him and he glared back. Joe's smile evaporated, no room for friendliness here. This was a different world.

It was not a particularly cold day, but some of the other new soldiers in the line up could not stop their teeth from chattering. They were clearly terrified of the unknown. Even the ones who were probably renowned on their own territories for being somewhat 'hard core', were having great difficulty showing off their 'machoism' here. "Ah!" thought Joe, "what will be has to be. Cannot alter anything now. Got to do it, so get on with it".

After a lot of shouting about what they were there for, and what they would have to do, a sorry lot of lads were marched quickly over to the supply depot for kitting out.

There they were issued with everything that they could possibly need in the way of basic clothing requirements. Battledress, uniforms and rifles, but no ammunition, and then promptly marched again to the quarters where they were to be billeted.

There they were met by the sergeant major and he lost no time in giving them instructions with no loving words. They were well and truly incarcerated in the army now.

Reveille was at five hundred hours the following morning and after a hurried breakfast 'square bashing' training started, and continued, until seventeen hundred hours every day. Exercise drilling, marching, gun assembly, full kit parades, eight to ten mile marches with full kit. Repeated and repeated every day for one month and the only thing to alleviate the boring routine and the exhaustion, was being allowed to go into the mess in the N.A.A.F.I., from twenty one hundred hours until twenty one thirty hours, big deal, and then to bed with lights out by twenty two hundred hours. "Let me come home mum. I'll never complain again!"

After the first month of hard training, the parents of the new recruits were invited to be present at the passing out parades of their precious sons. They had seemed to enjoy the pomp and ceremony and all appeared to be proud as punch of their offspring, extolling their achievements far beyond their merits and much to the embarrassment of the young men who would have preferred to just get the matter over with, without any fuss from their adoring audience.

With that over and a long weekend leave to compensate, Joe found himself at home once again. His parents were eager to hear of his experiences in the camp and he was eager to get off out with his pals and feel the freedom without any restrictions from anyone. He was not disappointed.

He was disappointed, however, that those last few days had passed by so quickly. It was not that he was in awe of returning to the camp but that he was having such a great time here at home. If this type of fun was to be had every time he had furlough then he could look forward to future leaves with much pleasure. He had never ever been the centre of so much attention and admiration in his life before. He had never realised that he was so popular, and was enjoying the experience immensely.

He had to be sure to arrive back at Strensall Barracks before twenty two hundred hours on the Tuesday which he had managed very easily after cadging a lift from a passing lorry, which was to become somewhat of a ritual with the chaps from the camp over the next few months.

The morning after he arrived back he was given orders as to what type of work he would be undertaking during his stay there.

"You're a good reckoner up of sums aren't you Bullimore?" the sergeant had questioned abruptly and a little condescendingly.

"Sir", Joe had agreed with a quick salute.

"Then the ration stores it is for you me lad. You'll have plenty of working out to do so that your mind won't vegetate and seize up. Can't have your little grey cells giving up on you, can we?"

The sergeant pleased as punch with his little self then shrugged, turned and marched Joe over to the ration stores in quickstep. Pointing to a building he gruffly informed him that a warrant officer would be on hand to show him the procedure and then he would be on his own. Full responsibility. Boss of himself. For a short while at least. He still had to be a soldier first and foremost and he had better not forget.

Warrant Officer Blake was a woman, which was a big surprise to Joe. He had imagined, and expected a large man, stomping about bombastically issuing orders and showing his authority. Instead, Blake was a rather small and plump motherly looking lady with a fresh complexion and stumpy legs covered in thick lisle stockings, highly polished shoes and immaculate uniform. He had smiled at the officer and to his astonishment she glared back at him. She might have been a woman but his previous assessment of the officer's personality had not been wrong.

For all that though, Blake knew her stuff and her instructions were simple, clear and precise. She had charted most things and written down absolutely everything, including where she could be easily contacted should he ever have any problems when she was not around. He thanked her verbally but she was silent socially and her only words on departure had been, "Get on with it soldier". And so he did.

From March to October 1953, Joe did the same job, issuing rations for the cookhouse on a daily basis, according to how many soldiers were on the camp on any one day. Each man was allocated sixpence halfpenny a day for his ration cash allowance or R.C.A. from the N.A.A.F.I. stores, which included items like sugar, butter, jam, marmalade, tea etc., but the fresh meat, bread, flour, vegetables and hard tack biscuits had to be collected out of camp, from the central ordnance stores, and so Joe had to quickly learn how to drive a motor vehicle in order to drive over there. It was a good reason to leave the camp once a week for some kind of relaxing variation.

The 'mess' was stark and dimly lit. The tables set out with the barest essentials. Each soldier kept his own mess tin and cutlery, and queued in line without any fuss, as to who was first to be served their meal. Most turned their noses up at the food at first at what they were being served, but very soon failed to respond in any way as hunger took over from presentation, and the meal was soon swallowed with great alacrity, except of course, for the hard tack biscuits, which were excellent in food nutrition value but could not easily be eaten unless they were dunked for about five minutes to soften them. Most of those biscuits were fed to the dogs owned by the camp officers and never refused.

Barry, Frank and Ron were all Yorkshire lads, all very good humoured and extremely likeable. From the very first day they had all hit it off and become inseparable. Joe really appreciated their friendship. On certain evenings they would be allowed out of the camp into the local suburbs of the town, or into York itself, where they soon became part and parcel of the local pubs, especially the "Dog and Gun", where they enjoyed the hospitality of the locals and became acquainted with the girls in the community. They made friends especially with four lovely girls but made it perfectly plain from the start that the girls could not rely on any serious attachments with them as they had no intention of being committed at this stage in their soldiering, and so the girls accepted the fact and realised that their stay in the camp would only be for a short duration of time.

Off with the old and on with the new became their motto also, and so the eight of them settled in to having a good time in a proper way, which, no doubt the girls' parents appreciated as they had heard from experience that some of the relationships that the local girls had entered into had had catastrophic results.

Inevitably all the lads had nicknames. Barry, being short and stocky in build was 'Egg' for 'Egg on legs'. Ron was 'Rick', because of his enduring love of the film Casablanca, Frank was 'Blue Eyes', because of his subsequent commitment to all things Frank Sinatra and Joe was merely 'J.J', an abbreviation of Joe John which was his full christian name and one which he dearly wished to leave behind him from his childhood days when he was always given his full title.

Collectively, they were all the great pretenders because of the total enthusiasm they all shared whilst doing their soldiering, especially on training schemes when they would be taken into the deep countryside for days on end to practise war games and survival. In these times Joe was king, and found that he had a good head for leadership, which earned him a promotion at an early date, but made no difference whatsoever to his relationship with the other three, they merely made a joke of it as always.

In early October of that year, Lance Corporal J.J. Bullimore and his three comrades were issued instructions that after one weeks furlough, they were all to be sent to Berlin for a six month tour of that country. Their mothers were all sickened at the thought of their boys being sent so far away, but the lads were all looking forward to the adventure with eager anticipation. It would give them good experience and broaden their horizons, after all none of them had been very far away from home at that time, only to the local seaside resorts for annual holidays. Joe was the only one who had ventured further and had been as far as London, and that was only for the day with college for the Festival of Britain exhibition. His only other claims to fame were that he had flown from Manchester airport to Paris, France, to see his mother's cousin for a few days. Then of course, to the convention and holiday in the Isle of Man and finally Provence, in France with Keith, Gina and co., and he reckoned that he was one of the privileged ones at that.

They could not wait.

October in Berlin was much the same in climate as it was back home in Britain, but naturally the surroundings were very different. Many of the war ruins still remained but much work was being undertaken mostly by foreigners, many of them British and Dutch, to rebuild the shattered city, and try to renovate and keep the old buildings for posterity which had a history and must not be lost if at all possible.

Any personal relationships undertaken with the German people were varied. Some were still repressing aggressive and hostile thoughts but the majority were trying to be at least amiable and looking forward optimistically to a brighter future. Most were just grateful to be living in western Berlin, and indeed, western Germany, instead of the oppressive eastern block, which was totally administered and dominated by the Soviets and ruled with an iron hand.

Even in Germany, Joe found himself still in charge of the ration stores, which was run pretty much the same as it had been at Strensall, although he did still have periods of guard duty along with other men.

One experience he would never forget was when he had to take his turn on being on guard at the notorious Spandau prison, where Rudolph Hess was incarcerated and would be for the rest of his natural life. He was the sole inmate of such a large institution, which was also the billet for numerous soldiers all guarding such a lone, once formidable deputy and right hand man of Adolph Hitler, the latter being the most notorious and evil tyrant in modern history. Looking at Hess it was very difficult to believe that this now pathetic man, with no future, was so important and powerful in the days of the Third Reich.

Joe would always remember his look. The square jaw, the steely blue eyes, the stoop of his shoulders and the sheer hopelessness shown in his stance.

The British soldiers took one monthly guard duties over him, followed by the Americans, French and Russians.

The winter months were harsh with deep snow drifting around the city streets and creating a dull quietness which hushed even the few vehicles that dared out in such inclement conditions.

The German people seemed well equipped for such weather, donning fur boots and thick coats and hats, looking more like Russians than anything else as they scurried about the streets at all times of the day and night.

The city never seemed to sleep. The night clubs opened for the young people until very late because they had never known the thrill of enjoyment before the war, and were making the most of it before they had to settle down and raise their own families in the future.

The local fraus usually kept themselves to themselves, but the young frauleins were usually quite flirtatious with the occupying forces, many of them marrying the foreign lads and happily moving back to Britain with them as their spouses when the lads returned.

Joe never failed to be perplexed by this as he felt that they would all still be alienated so soon after the war had ended. It was a good attitude but puzzling.

The tour of Germany had included trips to other cities such as Dusseldorf, Munich, Frankfurt and even the capital city of Bonne, which had been adopted as the capital since the war, as Berlin was now in three sectors.

Joe and his three pals had spent a wonderful two weeks furlough in the Swiss Alps, Austria, Bavaria and the Black Forest regions, where they had met and made, many friends from Germany, Switzerland and Austria, and had exchanged names and addresses with a promise to keep in touch, which of course he never had, and which he now regretted.

The tour had been over all too soon for Joe and the others and with another stripe on his sleeve, Corporal Bullimore left the Wevel camp at Spandau, and found himself back at Strensall Barracks, with a flat feeling of depression at losing all the excitement bestowed on him in the last six months.

The feeling thankfully did not last very long, he had much to tell his family and friends at home and a lot of catching up to do with his old pals. Keith was still writing regularly, but somehow they never did seem to get the respective leaves to coincide and so all their news had to be related by means of correspondence. Keith had joined the Guards and was now in the military police, in Trieste, Italy. Not a rank popular with the other soldiers but just up Keith's street as he had every intention of joining the police force once out of his National Service. He was a clever lad and felt the need to find his way into forensic investigations eventually.

According to his letters, the weather was always very clement in Italy, and the local signorinas very pleasing. Beyond that, Keith could say very little, being in a somewhat secret position. He would no doubt, enlighten him when they got together again one day when they would both swap stories about their respective experiences, but he did miss him. His 'soul mate'.

Meanwhile, Barry, Frank and Ron were still with him and that meant a lot to all of them.

……………………........

After a period of pistol training and more war games the lads were all sent to watch films on survival instructions once more, and shortly afterwards on to the medical centre for inoculation jabs, appertaining to tropical diseases.

Rumours and speculation as to where they were all being sent were rife, so soon after returning from Germany.

In June, 1954, a notice was pinned to the board with a list of men who would be embarking in three days time on the ship MV 'Georvic' from Liverpool, for a tour of Kenya, Africa.

Corporal J.J. Bullimore, Lance Corporal Barry Firth, Lance Corporal Frank Ineson and Lance Corporal Ronald Glover were all on that list.

The news was exciting, if a little scary as they were being sent to protect British ex patriots and other foreigners, especially the landowners, from that cruel sect known as the infamous Mau-Mau organisation led by a tribal chief called Jomo Kenyatta.

This was real. No more great pretenders, now they would be actually protecting others and looking out for themselves at the same time, a different carry on altogether.

Joe decided not to tell his parents where he was being sent to, until after he had actually gone. He would write and tell them. That way he would not have to see the look of panic on his mother's face.

With tropical kit and rifles well secured the men alighted from the train, which had taken them from York to Liverpool, where they had immediately embarked on the M.V. 'Georvic' in swift succession and without any mishaps whatsoever. They had been well trained.

The ship quickly sailed and the men were shown to their quarters and allocated their bunks. Joe was feeling queasy already from the swell created by the turning of the ship out of the dock. He swallowed hard but the saliva in his mouth kept on welling up. The ship's doctor was making his rounds and supplying dosages of sickness pills to anyone who felt the need. Most of the men did but they soon needed more when they reached the Bay of Biscay. The notorious swell of the sea was unbelievable as the cruel currents swirled and entwined in every direction. Joe had never seen so many different shades of grey and green on any one person's face before. The cook in the galley was having a day of rest as practically everyone was off his food for the duration of the trip across the bay.

Thankfully, as they cornered the Rock of Gibraltar and into the Mediterranean Sea, the water became calmer and the men were all getting quite used to the feel of the ship underneath them. By the time they had reached Port Said in Egypt, everyone seemed to be beginning to enjoy the trip.

They had had to wait in Port Said for a matter of twelve hours before they were allowed into the Suez Canal.

Because the wait was so short, they were not allowed to disembark, but they did enjoy seeing all the activity on the dockside, which was very different. The entertainment was provided by the local vendors selling their wares and all dressed in garb only seen by most of the soldiers in books and in films.

The sail down the Suez Canal was another, not to be forgotten experience. Most of the stone, used for the banking of the canal had been brought across from Cyprus. The British had a big hand in the engineering and construction of it, and Joe and the others had felt extremely proud and in awe of their achievement.

The banks of the canal were quite sheer, at which they had all felt some disappointment initially, as they had hoped to see more of Egypt on their way through. Nevertheless, in lots of ways they were not disappointed and were thrilled to find that among the sights and sounds were many local children standing on the banks and gleefully waving and shouting excitedly at seeing the foreign troops.

Their voyage had taken them on through the Red Sea and on to the Arabian Ocean, calling at Aden, a British Protectorate in the Yemen, but again only for six hours, until provisions had been loaded onto the ship, but for these six hours at least they were all allowed to disembark and look around the local market on the edge of the quayside. Naturally, they had all bought a few souvenirs and swapped many exciting stories once all back on board.

On again, they had sailed, on into the Indian Ocean and down the east coast of Africa. The lads had never known such hot weather and it would take some getting accustomed to. There would be no such thing as air conditioning where they would be going.

After twenty one days on the water and with only one six hour break on land, the ship eventually arrived in Mombasa, Africa. There was to be no overnight stay, so the men were quickly ushered from the ship and onto a train. With kit bags and equipment all firmly placed in overhead racks, the men endeavoured to settle down on the wooden slatted seats, which had never seen upholstery. The seats were extremely cruel on the hind sides of the soldiers after such a long and gruelling journey, even though naturally, they could all appreciate the reason for the lack of upholstery, as any coverings of that kind would have encouraged the nasty spiders and other little creatures to inhabit the inviting furl.

Passing through the countryside provided a wonderful spectacle. Lots of space.

Rolling hills and valleys. Little reed huts were dotted here and there, providing shelter for the colourful natives who were all going about their daily tasks. It was as though they had all the time in the world. No one hurried. It was far too hot. Everyone turned on hearing the sound of the train, and waved so excitedly one would have thought that this was the very first time that they had ever seen a one. Joe felt that they must have all been instructed to ingratiate themselves to the travellers.

Occasionally, the train would slow down almost to a halt at a junction, or actually stop altogether to take on board fuel and water. At these times, the local children would invariably beg or try to barter their wares, especially to the soldiers, whom they knew and remembered from past experience would buy souvenirs and perhaps give money for their pleasure.

The sunrise and the sunsets were so spectacular in colour they had to be experienced to be believed. The men had taken so many photographs over the past twenty one days it was doubtful that they would have film left for the rest of their tour of duty.

It took two days from Kilindini in Mombasa to reach the Nanyuki Camp which was to be their base camp for the duration of their eight month stay in Kenya. The whole trip had been undertaken without any complications or minor mishaps. Once installed into the camp there was no such thing as a 'sleep in' the following day to enable them all to catch up on their normal sleep pattern, which they might have lost during their long train journey.

Up at bugle call at five hundred hours the following day and after ablutions and breakfast, out on parade by six hundred hours in full tropical kit, already sweating profusely from the rising heat the soldiers had looked worn and literally fit to drop on the spot, but, if the sergeant noticed he never gave any indication.

All the soldiers were then informed that they were now to be attached to the Royal Signal Regiment, and communications would be a definite objective and serious issue from now on.

Joe had fully expected to be in charge of the stores as always, but instead he was given the permanent job of telephone switchboard operator, which he would be designated to do for the rest of his tour of Kenya. He was pleasantly pleased. It would make a refreshing change and he was quite looking forward to it.

Over the next months everything went smoothly and efficiently. No real calamities. They went out on patrols but there was never any real combat. They had all expected to be confronted at some time by machete knife-wielding terrorists but the only real Mau-Mau they saw were the ones who had been captured by other soldiers, arrested and brought to their camp for interrogation. Some of the actual Kikuyu tribe even worked alongside them in the camp with other natives. They all appeared to be quite normal, and not aggressive, but the soldiers had all been indoctrinated not to trust anyone, as some of the tribesmen could be infiltrating to obtain information to take back to the Kenyatta base.

Training schemes were still compulsory but even though they were very hard work they were also extremely enjoyable. The men were taken many miles away from the Nanyuki camp and much further into the interior where the countryside was vast and appeared limitless.

At Mount Kenya they settled into Ngobit camp and climbed parts of the Abadair Mountains, as part of their stealth training, which was cruel and exhausting work but gave them all leg muscles like iron and made them discover that they had stamina that they never knew they had.

For something a little lighter later on in the scheme they were all taken to stay at the Carnegie farm, owned by white landowners, where they were made wholly welcome and treated well in gratitude for their protection.

From there they patrolled the Nyere Township, ensuring that there was no infiltration to menace or intimidate the townsfolk into joining their evil groups or of them being hurt or afraid of the Mau-Mau organisation themselves.

Joe and his three pals had been fortunate to be able to stay together on that tour and were all equally as eager to see as much of the beautiful Kenyan countryside as they could whilst they had the opportunity of being there.

Their ambition was to visit the Masai Mara National Park, to see and live with the big cats for a few days, or visit Lake Victoria, or even Turtle Bay on the coast, which was reputed to be like paradise, but those experiences never materialised as any kind of normal tourism was far too dangerous. They were, however, all determined to try and return one day to realise those dreams.

All the soldiers had many experiences in the duration of their stay. Joe distinctly remembered arriving back into the camp after a short leave in the country's capital, Nairobi, and sitting in his telephone communications unit when he had heard an enormously loud humming sound coming from outside and he was not the only one. Every door of every billet had opened in unison to investigate the alien sounds. Their eyes had widened with extreme astonishment at what they saw.

Rising from the ground in their millions were termites. Flying ants, unseen in such multitudes before but so thick and so dense that eventually the other side of the camp was obliterated from sight altogether. The noise became louder and louder by the second. There seemed to be no end to them. They were not attacking anyone, but where they were going was a complete enigma. The men had never been forewarned that such a thing could happen, and had no idea at all of what the consequences would be.

Men were scattered about, batting off the creatures from their faces and bodies as they collided, not biting or harming, just going, but to where?

The humming never ceased for a full four hours, and then, just as quickly as it had started, the noise ceased and a complete silence ensued for a few minutes until the usual drone and click of the grasshoppers in the tall grasses started again to take its place.

The camp soon got back to normality. A native lad

brought in a cup of tea, his broad smile brightening up his face from ear to ear, his perfectly formed white teeth flashing in the darkness like pure ivory as he realised that their experience was a first for all the soldiers on this tour and was very pleased with himself to think that he knew more than they did of the facts behind the incident.

In pigeon English he spoke and motioned for them to listen again, and sure enough another noise began to rumble down at the camp but a very different noise from the last one. Thunder.

The heavens opened. Before even ten minutes had elapsed the whole of the camp was ankle deep in water. The deluge resulted in torrents of water rushing into the camp from everywhere possible in great streams, creating rivers of debris in its wake. The lightening was like the men had never seen before and the thunder continued to rumble on for what seemed like an eternity but must have been for no more that a few minutes in all, before it spent itself and stopped.

Survival. The termites certainly knew what they were about. They were surely seeking out higher ground. Nature, intelligence! Who said we homo sapiens had the greatest brainpower on the planet?

After the storm had subsided, the air had remained fresher for the next few days, which was a refreshing relief, but then the ground became so dry again, it was difficult to believe that there had ever been a storm at all.

Nairobi was explored twice more before the eight month tour was over and Frank and Ron had fallen completely in love with the country altogether, so much so that they pledged that when their National Service was over they were both going to try and return and join the Kenyan Police force and make their lives there.

Joe recalled that if that had been his and Barry's wish,

the dream could not have been realised as they never reached the required height called for by the force.

When the tour was over the men were instructed that they would not be returning home by sea. They were informed that they were to fly.

Consequently, on their return journey their aircraft had touched down, and called in at Entebbe in Uganda, but only for a short stop in order to refuel. They had then flown on to Khartoum, in the Sudan, and then on to Naples in Italy for the same reasons, before touching down in London.

The rest of journey was by train from London to Strensall, York, and it was winter but it was grand to be home. Joe knew that much as he had enjoyed his stint in the forces and the trips abroad, his roots were here and would never ever be anywhere else.

Chapter Four

"Joe John Bullimore, I don't believe it!"

The voice rained down at him from above as he quickly tried to regain his composure. He gazed upward but the sun was bright and blinded him leaving only a shadow silhouette of a woman at his side. He raised a cupped hand to shield his eyes but the woman stepped around to face him realising his plight.

"You don't recognise me, do you?" she said with a knowing grin stretching from ear to ear but she was so obviously pleased to see him.

Joe screwed his eyes up still attempting to accustom them to the light. "You will have to excuse me, I think I fell asleep and I am still a little dazed, I feel rather stupid I'm afraid". He still felt rather rude even after the apology. "I have got to say though, that I do know your face very well but don't exactly recognise you and am still trying to place you, sorry".

The smart looking woman looked about his age, medium height with striking grey eyes and short honey blonde hair, which curled ever so slightly into light flicks around her neck. Her skin was flawless with hardly a wrinkle and only showing the laughter lines around her attractive face.

"Well Joe, we have all grown much older since we two last met, but I would like to think that I am still recognisable". She was joking and making light of it all and was smiling broadly again obviously trying to put him at his ease and knowing that she had jolted him out of his sleep and did not wish to embarrass him further. Then her eyes widened in anticipation as she saw the look of realisation and recognition flood across his face.

"Maddie!" Joe leapt from the bench with sincere and obvious delight. He wrapped his arms around her and pecked her affectionately on the cheek. "Maddie!" he repeated, "You can't know how good it is to see you. My goodness, it must be … how long?"

"It has got to be over thirty years I know", she said with a sincere hint of sadness which could not be mistaken, showing in her voice, "but it is so good to see you again after all this time. I had heard some time ago that you had returned to Yorkshire to live and I did think that I might have seen you around but I never did. There must be so many things to talk about, the two of us after so many years".

"You bet there is". Joe answered in response. "We will have to get together and have a real old chat sometime".

Maddie's face straightened for a second and showed some concern, for only a moment lest he became aware of her reaction. She smiled again and said "I had seen you sitting here on this bench over an hour ago when I came into the park but did not take much notice, then when you were still here, and more or less in the same position I became a little concerned thinking that perhaps you were ill. I decided to come over to see if you were alright and offer you a cup of tea in the Club house. It was only when I came over here that I realised it was you. I could not believe it. You are not ill are you Joe?"

"No, love", Joe answered a little too quickly, "I'm not ill at all just a bit short of something to do and trying to lose a bit of time. Not that we should want to lose any time, we have all little enough at our time of life. I just got carried away with my thoughts and must have inadvertently nodded off. I feel rather foolish now, all I can hope is that not many people took notice, apart from you that is. I am really pleased that you did, otherwise I would never have met up with you again. What are you doing then in this clubhouse?"

"Well, I have been a team player and member of the crown green bowls team in the park for quite a few years now, well that is, me and my Frank. I don't actually play much these days. I do come, however, to make the teas, coffee's, sandwiches and cakes when it is my turn, and today it is my turn and so here I am". She outstretched her arms and smiled broadly again. "Are you coming with me for a cup of tea then or aren't you? If you are, then follow me".

She turned and skipped lightly like a young girl towards the neat clubhouse in the far corner of the green. Joe with a good feeling, obediently and joyfully followed her, her obvious enthusiasm and vitality rubbing off on him every step of the way.

Some of the men had already laid down their bowls and the room was humming with chatter, laughter and activity. The cups were clattering, and the sandwiches were being devoured with great gusto. After a moment of quiet, to see who the stranger at the door might be everyone in turn greeted him with cheerful responses of "Good morning", etc., and after a few courteous nods Joe restricted himself to the rear of the clubhouse not wanting to be felt intrusive. Maddie, with her natural cheerfulness introduced him as a long lost friend, whom she had not seen for over thirty years, and after a few raised eyebrows and comments like, "You'll have a lot to catch up on then", they were left alone.

After all the pots were washed, and the place tidied up, they quickly locked up and started up the path to make their way out of the park.

Maddie groped about in her bag for her car keys and asked if she could give Joe a lift.

"No I don't think so", Joe answered politely.

"Why, have you got your own car here?" she seemed surprised at his refusal.

"Oh no, it isn't that, I left the car at home because I felt the need to walk, but, at the same time I haven't quite decided where I want to go, or even what I wish to do as yet, and so if I carry on walking I might just come to some decision". His face was sombre, and his final sentence trailed off, as he noticed some kind of quizzical expression cross Maddie's face.

Her face bereft of smile now looked up at him with real concern. "Joe, you are not really being straight with me, are you? There is something wrong and I know it. I know it is ages since we saw each other but you can confide in me if you want to you know. I would be happy to listen, I am very discreet. Are you ill?"

Joe sighed deeply, and knew that she had noticed, as she was very observant. He took her by the elbow and led her to the car, smiling all the while, as if to pacify her, but she was not about to be shook off. She was like a dog with a bone.

He submitted. "O.K. Maddie, the truth is that I am a bit low, fed up, depressed a little, sick of my life, and wondering where on earth I am going. The devil is in the detail, and I cannot, and will not, pester you or anyone else with those details. The solution is in my own hands and I will have to deal with it. I always have before".

She tried to smile to make him feel better but she knew that that would be too patronising and futile, that what he needed most of all at this time was someone to talk to. To bear his soul to. To off load his troubles and get them out of his system. He had made it perfectly clear that he did not wish to discuss the problem but she could try very slowly to coax him. What had she to lose? He had everything to gain.

"You know Joe, you should be in 'the pink!' You should be retiring early and enjoying your leisure and travelling to all kinds of places. Places you must have always wanted to visit, it could be a big, new adventure".

Joe could not control the sarcasm in his voice in response to her words. "I should be", he retorted, not angry with her, "but if you are going to colour me anything at all, then colour me 'Blue'. Definitely blue".

"Well, we shall have to do something about that then Joe, won't we? If you do not know what you are going to do with your day, and where you are going, then I shall take over your day. I am a bit of a lost soul myself some days and today is one of those days. I suggest that you get into my car and follow the guide who will lead you into a magical, mystical world of conversation and intrigue".

Her eyes were wide at her pretence of jollifications. She made him laugh. She had not changed. Always the clown. He did as she ordered and stepped into the car. He did not know it but she was not clowning now, she was deadly serious. Her old friend was in deep trouble. She knew it, but he obviously did not, and she was determined to do something about it before it was too late. She turned on the ignition and steered the car downhill, towards the centre of the town, with Joe at her side innocently oblivious of what she had in mind.

Maddie parked the car at the parking meter in the centre of the town and then turned to speak to Joe. "I have to call into the chemist for a prescription for a neighbour and I need some bread from the bakery, after that the remainder of the day is ours. Do you want to stay in the car or shall I meet up with you in about half an hour?"

"I will meet you in half an hour because whilst we are here I may as well pick up some paints for my water colour painting. I am running short and I could also do with a newspaper".

They both alighted. Maddie quickly locked the car and took off like a whirlwind soon to be lost in the crowd down the busy precinct.

All chores done by both of them, and back in the car in less than half an hour later Maddie started the car again and drove off. "I think the first thing we will do is go and eat. I would like to bet that you have not had a proper meal today have you?"

"Well, I have had some toast for breakfast and those sandwiches at the club, but to tell you the truth I haven't felt very hungry", Joe answered quietly.

"Well, I know that you like fish, I remember that!" she said obviously very proud of her excellent memory.

"How on earth do you remember that?" Joe's eyebrows lifted in an expression of bewilderment.

"Do you remember when we were young? Well, you had an aunt and uncle who lived in Grimsby and they used to send you fresh fish by rail. It was all tied up securely in a hessian carrier bag and you took me once or twice to collect it from the railway station. Your mother, always so very generous to us, used to give us some of it, knowing that we needed the vitamins and you used to devour yours saying that it was your favourite food. Yes, I remember so well".

"You astonish me Maddie, all those little minor and really insignificant details, I can hardly believe it".

"Well now, I am going to take you to a wonderful little

fish restaurant which has opened only quite recently. It is divine, and is situated only at the top of the Salandine, off Calder Beck, and we can be there in two ticks".

Sure enough, Maddie had hardly uttered the words when she was driving into the newly tarmac covered car park.

The restaurant looked purpose built and Joe gasped a little as they entered the establishment. It was not like any fish restaurant he had ever seen before. Beautifully decorated in a very tasteful manner. Crystal chandeliers hanging from the ceiling, cosy romantic wall lights and fresh, crisp and clean pink linen on the tables. Silver cruets, sugar bowls and milk jugs, tiny posies of fresh Freesias centre table and delicate fine white bone china crockery.

A well dressed young man, in black and white attire was standing in the corner beside the bar and came over immediately. He showed them to their table and swiftly took their orders. He smiled sincerely and cheerfully and stated that they were just in time as they offered reduced rates for pensioners before five o'clock.

"For pensioners!" Joe teased, "but we are not pensioners, we're only thirty eight".

Joe had expected the young waiter to shuffle and shyly apologise but instead he went along with the teasing and quickly replied, "Well sir, then you must have had a very hard life. My commiserations". With an impish expression, he turned, and went off with their order.

Maddie was delighted to see that Joe was relaxing enough to be able to joke. She remembered that in the old days he used to have razor sharp wit, but she was not going to remind him of that at this time as it might send him back into the shell that he now appeared to be crawling out of, albeit, ever so slowly.

The meal was served within five minutes. A considerable sized battered haddock sizzling hot from the pan, and chipped potatoes served with a green salad garnish. Very well presented and appetising to behold. A silver carousel with tartare sauce, tomato ketchup, relish sauces and chutney were placed in the centre of the table. Cold butter curled on a tiny silver salver was provided for the fresh warm crusty brown and white rolls in the basket.

It was heavenly not to have to use those silly sachets of condiments and sugars. So simple but so effective.

They started to eat, then Joe looked at Maddie and said, "How come that you are at a loose end today then Maddie, is Frank at work?"

Her eyes misted over but only for a second until she had quickly composed herself. She had known that the question would inevitably arise at some time but she had not expected it just at that moment.

"No Joe, I've lost him. He died two years ago".

Joe was silent for a little while. "I am so sorry Maddie. I had no idea. I wouldn't have said…I feel so badly about this".

Maddie reached out and placed her hand over his. "It's alright Joe, these things happen. I was going to tell you, I just hadn't got around to it that's all. Don't feel badly about it, I know most people are embarrassed and find that talking about such things are difficult but believe me it is alright to talk. I talk about him all the time. You cannot live with someone all that time and forget that they ever existed. Whether they are gone or not they still exist very strongly in your mind". She carried on eating and then paused again. "You know we had a wonderful marriage, no regrets. One just thinks that things will go on forever, and of course they never do. One is bound to go and leave the other one day. I just like to think that one day all the people we have loved, and who have gone, will be there waiting for us when it is our turn and we will all have a damned good party with no more worries or cares. I know I'm daft but that's me, and what I like to think will happen. You have got to keep the faith otherwise, well, what else is there?"

Joe nodded. "It's a good attitude Maddie and I am glad to know that you can feel that way. You had gone out with him from being very young hadn't you, I remember?"

Maddie's face lit up eager to talk about her late husband, but equally as eager for Joe to show some interest in her life. "Yes, we were both only seventeen but I didn't start out feeling at all serious about him". She giggled to herself wondering whether or not to tell Joe about her little infatuation, and then decided to indulge herself and reveal her little secret, as it might just amuse him. "You know what Joe, it was you that I fancied. I had this thing about you. I used to stand on street corners when I knew you would be passing and I would haunt places where I knew you would be. I even started going to your church and learned how to ring the bells, a bit of campanology eh? I used to think that you looked like Richard Todd and he was my screen idol. Of course, I knew that you never knew. You were always very pleasant and polite to me, and always stopped to talk, but you never had any inclination that I was standing there, my poor heart doing somersaults, and my knees shaking all the while".

Joe giggled back. "I did know, you know, but I never let on. I didn't want to encourage you. When we are young a two year age gap means a lot and I just thought that you were just having a schoolgirl crush that you would soon outgrow. I have got to say that I was flattered, lads usually are, though, they would never ever admit it at the time".

"If I had only known!" she feigned a gesture of despair and then continued, "but, well Frank lived at the other end of our street and he was always hanging around me. I wasn't in the least bit interested as he had a spotty face and wasn't quite as tall as I was. I have to laugh now though because he dosed himself with lots of concoctions, raw onions, ground nutmeg in milk, garlic and many other old wives' remedies in order to rid himself of the teenage acne. I don't know if any one of them worked but the rash did eventually go and his skin was perfect after that. He obtained a job as an apprentice mechanic when he left college. It was just a one man business but of course when he finished his apprenticeship he had to go away and serve his National Service like you all did, but he made me promise to write to him regularly, which I did, but you know Joe I missed him so much, I would never have believed it. He went away and when he returned he had grown several inches and broadened out and was quite the muscle man and very dishy. I fell in love…. Do you want me to go on, am I boring you?"

Joe found himself abstractly doodling on the table napkin with his finger nail, so intently was he listening to her revelations. "Of course not. Do go on, I am very interested to know what happened to you".

Maddie seemed pleased at his reaction. It was good to talk about the old days both for him and for her.

"Well I had quite a decent job working in the booking office at the railway station and I had managed to save quite a tidy sum of money and so we decided to get married. We were going to buy a small terrace house at the other end of town and were anticipating setting a date for the wedding. That's when the bombshell came".

Joe remained silent only raising a thick bushy eyebrow which she interpreted as being eager to know what was to follow, and so continued.

"The owner of the garage where Frank worked had a very bad heart attack and the doctors all said that he would never be able to work again. The garage would have to be sold and there would be no guarantee that the new owners would be able to employ Frank. However, Mr Swailes approached Frank and made him a proposition. Would he like to have first option of buying the garage? He would give him first refusal and was offering to lend him the money. If he did, then Mr Swailes would allow him to pay off the loan personally over the next five years without interest and could he let him know within the next few days?"

She paused now to check and see if she was boring Joe, and after seeing him beckon her to go on, she continued. "Well, Frank came to see me at my mother's house and told me all about it but we could see no way of being able to buy the garage. In the meantime it was more than likely that Frank would lose his job. How could we get married and be able to pay the mortgage?

That was when my mother entered into the conversation. She was prolific and confidently said that we could do it, and to quote her she said, 'speculate to accumulate, I have always taught you. What you do, is use the monies that you were going to use as a deposit for your house as a deposit for the garage, and either wait a year or so to get married or come to live here with me until you are able save up enough again to get your own house. That way you will not only have a job, but you will be self employed, with a business which you already know is established, profitable and an ongoing concern', unquote.

Maddie smiled wistfully as she recalled the obvious and ongoing wisdom of her mother. "She was wonderful, my mum, and always worth listening to, because as you remember when my father was so very ill and housebound, they had had no option but to sell his cobblers shop. It would have been very easy for her to whittle away the money from the business as she had to support herself and my father and four children. She could not go out to work to earn and so she improvised. She used the money from the shop and bought as many items of food from the wholesalers as she could"…

"She set up a house shop in your front parlour. Yes, I remember", Joe interrupted her in full stream. "As I remember she did very well".

"She did", agreed Maddie. "We were never going to be wealthy but we did alright. It meant that mum could be at home when we arrived home from school and she never had to leave dad".

"So is that what you did, you and Frank, bought the garage?" Joe inquired.

"Yes we did. I am not going to say that it was easy. Frank worked all hours putting most of the money he made back into the business. I carried on working, and saving my wages for the little house we were determined to have one day. Anyway, at the end of four years Frank was employing two more qualified mechanics and an apprentice. The garage was paid for and we had moved into our little terrace house.

We had always wanted to buy a cottage. You know, the type that is a bit derelict that can be done up to suit yourself, and we had never been able even to consider it before, but now we could. We found this dilapidated one at the far side of the town cradled in a little niche in the Pennine hills. It had great potential as far as we could see but needed a lot of money spending on it. So back again we went, remembering mother's philosophy. We sold the terrace house and bought a caravan for five hundred pounds, and parked it in the garage yard. Again I carried on working, and every week we bought materials and every week we worked every spare second, and with the help of some good friends started at the top and worked down to the bottom. The kitchen sink was stone, shallow and gritty, with brass taps that were green and mouldy, surrounded by blue and white tiles all hair cracked. The bathroom was horrible. The bath being on four legs, which I believe now to be quite fashionable again, was rusty and filthy. I would not have even stood up to wash in it let alone sit in it.

It took us almost two years to finish the house even with the help of the precious friends. We were sincerely grateful to them and will always be indebted to them. Then there was the garden, which was in a terrible state, but we employed someone to do all the grafting and hard work as we were at the stage where we could not face any more of it by then, but it was worth it. We have lived there ever since and have loved every minute of being there.

You know, we sold the caravan for the same price as we had paid for it, and that five hundred pounds, bought us the rest of the furniture we needed."

Joe lifted his face from the table and directed his eyes straight at her showing his admiration for their courage and endeavours. "I really think that is marvellous, Maddie. I never had such incentives. You have got to have both parties concerned in the same mind to be able to make things like that work. I never was so fortunate".

His eyes had misted over and Maddie had noticed and heard every word he had said and absorbed them. It was the first time that he had ever made any reference to his marriage at all but it was too early in their conversation to broach it any further and so she purposely decided to ignore it, for the moment anyway.

"The house was so lovely, and we were so proud of it, but once we were installed we decided that now was the time to start a family. Well, we tried and tried, and nothing happened, and then after two years I finally became pregnant. We were ecstatic but we lost the baby. I miscarried at three months and to cut a story short, in the next five years I lost three babies in all.

When I reached thirty, we decided that enough was enough, and that we should try to adopt. We completed all the paperwork and went to all the interviews and then one day I was out shopping and felt shocking. So ill, and had no idea what was wrong with me. I searched for a seat to sit myself down but never reached one. I passed out. The next thing I knew I was being carted away to hospital.

My blood pressure was very high, and at first they thought that perhaps I had suffered a slight stroke, but after many tests the doctor finally came to see me and said that my condition was caused by my being five months pregnant. I almost had a stroke then I can tell you, it was such a shock but such a delight to find out, although I still had enough sense to be cautious because of my past history, and did as advised and rested for all the rest of my pregnancy".

"So you have children then Maddie?" Joe exclaimed with obvious delight.

"No Joe. Not children. I have one daughter. I never did have more children but she is such a delight and always has been. She is twenty eight years old now and married and a career but she doesn't live very far away and I see her very often. We are very close, it is wonderful".

After a short pause in the conversation when they sipped the last drops of their tea, which was by now cold. Joe motioned to his watch and pointed out the time. "Do you realise how long we have been here? I think we had better be making tracks or they will be asking us to leave".

Maddie nodded in agreement and started to rise from the chair. Joe made sure that he reached the bar in order to pay the cheque before she could attempt to do so. The pleasant young man politely asked if everything had been satisfactory and Joe complimented him on the standard of the restaurant and food, mentioning old world standards, and assured him that they would visit again before too long. With that they both left and got back into the car once more.

…………………….......

Joe turned to look at Maddie as she confidently drove off from the restaurant. He had the distinct impression that she had far more up her sleeve than she was about to admit. Nevertheless, it was lovely being with her and he decided that he would humour her and see what transpired.

It was about a half hour drive to Maddie's house, and on arrival, she carefully turned into the drive and pulled on the handbrake.

To the left of them stood this quaint and very pretty cottage type house with a solid oak Jacobean style door situated in the centre, and sporting a gigantic brass knocker, the door being housed inside an open porch, covered with sweet smelling honeysuckle, and all built of the local Pennine stone, quarried locally years ago, and still blackened from the many years of textile soot drifting over during the industrial revolution.

Joe felt that it would have spoiled the look of the house, had it been sandblasted clean.

"Well, we are here. I thought it would be rather nice on such a lovely day to spend some time in the garden, at least until a little later. Come on I will show you".

She led him gently by the elbow down the original

cobbled courtyard filled with moss covered pots all planted with different shrubs now opening their newly budded leaves in the late Spring sunshine. They cornered the pretty little house and the garden opened up into a long lawn surrounded by flowers of every colour and hue, looking like they had all just been scattered there haphazardly, but had obviously been planted with some thought to give that impression. The taller plants all at the rear and the smaller plants all intermingling in sizes and bordering off with numerous varieties of Hostas. At the bottom of the large garden was a natural stream, crystal clear, and swiftly falling straight down from the Pennine hills, tumbling over rocks and stones and the water scintillating in the late afternoon sunshine.

Joe just stood there, watching the birds and the butterflies and three small rabbits scuttling about on the hillside. He was lost for words. The flora and the fauna. It was so lovely. He thought of Frank and wished he had known him. He had toiled all his life and had everything he could possibly have wanted, love, comfort, happiness and then dying and having to leave it all so prematurely, just when he should have been enjoying every moment of the fruits of his labours.

"You like my garden then Joe?", Maddie whispered coming up from behind him. "The water is pure you know, I've had it tested. I sometimes come out for a glassful. Perhaps I could bottle it, I might make a fortune", she jested.

"I was just thinking Maddie, what a sickening shame it is that Frank had so much, not just materially, but the fact that you were happy, content and comfortable and he has had to leave it all behind. It's more than a shame it is diabolically tragic. What really is the point to it all?" he said suddenly feeling a little angry, but still very sad and morose.

Maddie looked at Joe but he did not meet her eyes. She knew that he was quite distressed and guessed that it was not just with thoughts of Frank and tried to pacify him. "I always think that we all come into this world with nothing and we all go out the same way, but it is what you do with the middle part that counts and even though Frank worked very hard he did enjoy the time he had. He would have no regrets. I know that."

Joe turned away in order to compose himself. It was becoming too easy these days to show his emotions, and he did not like that feeling of nudity. He had to use all his self control to conceal it. He was not entirely oblivious of the fact that Maddie was watching him so intently, and that she had noticed how his shoulders were so drooped with despair. That his hands were constantly fisted with obvious anger and frustration and that he was all the while distinctly uneasy even in her company.

"You haven't built a conservatory yet then Maddie?" he said wishing desperately to turn the conversation around before she could scrutinise him more.

"No I don't like them really. I think that they will be over hot in the summer and very cold in the winter and all that glass to keep clean! But of course, everyone does what they want. It is up to the individual I think. Why do you have one Joe?"

"No, we don't, but I know many people do nowadays. I thought it was the norm at the moment. You know the modern trend to go like the Victorians?" He shrugged, and laughed at the way everything appeared to go in circles, varied but initially the same.

"Well, we do have the French-style windows which open out onto the patio, and we sit underneath the pergola, and that is well covered with Clematis and so it is shaded. I don't really like sitting out in the direct sunlight, and if it is not fit to sit outside I just open the windows and sit in the lounge, taking in the fresh air from there. The air is so sweet and it suits me fine".

Joe looked around with obvious interest. The patio was like everything else, neat and tidy with a dark green cast iron table and chairs, all set out ready to accommodate any visitors, of which he thought there would be many.

She followed him down the garden path and beckoned him to follow her into the house "Come on, we'll go inside and make a drink. Tea or coffee or anything else?" she enquired.

"I will have a coffee thanks. I think I must be addicted", he said lightly, "If I go too long without caffeine I get withdrawal symptoms". He was joking again. Now his moods fluctuated at random but Maddie was more than willing to pander to him. So she unlocked the door and led him into the kitchen.

Joe looked around still with admiration. This was the type of house he could settle in. The walls were all rustic brick with a dark green, gleaming clean, Aga cooker nestling into an inglenook. Deep mullioned windows, all separately diamond paned were framed by deep wine coloured chintz curtains. A creel hung from the ceiling adorned with dried herbs, garlic bulbs and dried flowers. Jam pans and Chinese woks hung from the ceiling hooks but within easy reach. On the matt, rustic ceramic tiles on the floor stood beautifully carpentered dark oak units, with a welsh dresser tucked into a recess filled with blue and white Italian spode crockery. He was full of admiration for their excellent taste and could not refrain from telling her so because the cosy lived in feeling of the house made him feel warmly contented.

"I thought you would like it. I can remember that your mother liked blue and white crockery and ornaments and that she collected quite a lot of Dutch Delftware".

"She did!" Joe exclaimed in amazement. "I wonder what else you will be reminding me of. The mind boggles".

With the coffee percolator plugged firmly into its socket, Maddie ushered him through into the dining room and lounge. "I don't usually show anyone around but seeing that you are so obviously enjoying the house, I will".

Joe was not disappointed. This house was so much a home and not a showpiece. Again a rustic fireplace and open log fire with brass and copper pieces all shiny and bright placed strategically here and there. Dried flower arrangements on the hearth. Oak beamed ceilings and windows still mullioned and diamond paned, framed by the same dark claret chintz as the window seats and suite. Dark antique Jacobean and Tudor style furniture placed perfectly in both rooms with tasteful reading lamps on small occasional tables making reading easy and again the blue and white china pieces on different cabinets and shelves. The dining table was able to accommodate at least eight, and was centred with a bowl full of fresh anemones. The table surrounded by three dining chairs on either side and one carver chair at each end, all high backed and covered in real dark red leather, everything sitting on a thick deep red carpet which almost swallowed up his feet.

Maddie rushed off back to the kitchen, through the latted door, furnished with cast iron latches and hinges, to pour out the coffee and asked if he would prefer a cup or a beaker. He said he would have a beaker and not to stand on ceremony for him.

She appeared at the door with a delicate fluted china beaker in each hand. "Would you rather stay inside or go back out into the garden? Only, it does seem to be dropping rather cool out there and when you are sitting you can feel a bit chilled".

"I will do anything that you want to do", Joe replied, content to do absolutely anything she wished.

With that comment Maddie proceeded to sit down in the nearest chair and he levered himself into the chair opposite. "So you thought I looked like Richard Todd did you?" he said pretending to mock and with his face showing a comical expression but clearly flattered. Then he threw his head back and laughed. "I wonder if I still do. At least you recognised me and so I can't have altered all that much. Have I?"

"No you haven't changed all that much Joe, you are still easily recognisable. You still have very good teeth and of course that very cute dimple in your chin, but there is just one thing that strikes me, and that is your eyes".

"My eyes?" Joe repeated after her, suspicious of what she was going to say, and hoping that it would not be what he thought.

"Yes, your eyes used to dance with mischief and even when you tried to be straight faced your eyes gave you away because they were still twinkling and laughing". She looked directly at him waiting for his response. She was not disappointed.

"So now?" he said pointedly but with an indication that he knew exactly what she was going to say.

"Now, they are dull and sad and I keep looking for the laughter brimming up but even when you smile your eyes remain the same. You know, Joe, the eyes are the windows of the soul and I can tell that you are not a happy man".

Joe shrugged but smiled "How long have you been a philosopher?"

"Just that little old thing called common sense that's all", she answered, determined to get to the bottom of his problem even though she knew she would have to act with some tact and diplomacy, and she might have to wait quite a while.

"Why did you give up working Joe, if you weren't ready?" Maddie asked with some concern.

"I didn't", Joe answered swiftly.

"Sorry, but I was under the impression that that is probably why you are at a loose end", Maddie said with pretended confusion showing in her voice.

"No, I should apologise for misleading you love. I did not give up work but I am not working. Work gave me up. I was made redundant a few months ago and it all came suddenly and was a great shock. I just was not ready that is all. I have tried to get other employment but I am afraid the employers take one look at your date of birth on the application form and then just lay it aside. Ageism. Let's face it at our age we are unemployable. I will still keep on trying though. I haven't much else to do, you never know, one day I may get lucky".

"What about doing your own job at home, surely you have clients you could still do accounts for?" Maddie suggested trying to encourage him.

"I would have only one problem there, in fact, I had many clients who asked me to continue auditing their books but it is not the money I need, Maddie. I must get out of the house. Meet other people. Socialise and the rest. If I stayed at home to work, I would be in isolation, and that would really drive me crazy", he explained.

"What type of work are you looking for Joe?" she asked hopefully.

"Anything, anything at all", he retorted showing his exasperation. "My qualifications are not relevant any more".

Maddie swallowed deeply hoping that she was not

going to offend him by her suggestion. "I have a proposition for you Joe".

He looked across at her in anticipation of what she was going to say, "Yes?"

"I will give you a job if you want one so badly", she offered. "We are wanting someone at the garage. Well it's a filling station really, they don't repair cars or anything like that".

"What kind of job" Joe asked his face lighting up at the prospect.

"Well, I never finished telling you my story. I'll just enlighten you and then you will understand. When Frank reached forty he started with quite bad arthritis and he couldn't do his job properly. He contacted a few petrol companies, and to cut a long story short he ended up selling his beloved motor garage and buying a petrol station. In the next ten years he had acquired three of them in different parts of the town and put managers in all of them. He had sold his other garage to his foreman. Just like Mr. Swailes had sold his to Frank. After Frank died I sold two of the filling stations to their respective managers and have only one left, and it is at that station that we are needing someone, just to take the money at the till for the petrol, fill up, and sell the items on the shelves". She waited to see if she could see any sign of indignation at her offer of such a maybe downgrading proposition, after all he was a fully qualified accountant with a degree of merit behind him.

"I cannot believe it. How absolutely wonderful", he exclaimed with so much joy he almost leapt from the chair. "Are you sure?", he ejaculated in disbelief at his good fortune.

"Absolutely. You can start tomorrow if you want to. I'll 'phone Jack Hillam first thing in the morning and tell him that you have taken the job, and to expect to see you around, what eleven o'clock? He is the manager, and I am sure that you will get along with him fine. He's a lovely chap. The only thing though Joe, there is a drawback".

Joe interrupted her in full stream, "Don't say that!".

"No Joe, I mean the hours. They are six hourly shifts. Four people do the job and some weeks you would work mornings, then afternoons, then evenings and nights. They are rather unsociable hours".

"I don't care about that. It is just so wonderful I can't tell you. But tell me why did you not sell all of the garages? Why just the two?" he questioned.

Maddie nestled herself further into the chair and prepared to relate the full story, happy in the fact that she could still see Joe on a regular basis. "Frank had already decided to work only a year or two more and he had got all his managers together and told them of his intentions.. The managers of two of the garages were only in their thirties with families and mortgages. He told them in good time so that they could make arrangements to buy the garages from him themselves. Now Jack was a different proposition. He was coming up to sixty years of age and going to be too old to buy and so Frank decided to keep that one garage until Jack wanted to retire, because if the new owners would not employ him he would be out of work and too young to receive a state pension, and just like you would have found it difficult to get another job. With Frank dying so suddenly, I wasn't really prepared and did not want the responsibility of the business. I took advice from our solicitor and decided to adhere to what Frank would have wanted. He attended to the matter in conjunction with our wishes. Now Jack runs the business and very ably too, I do not have any worries on that score and everyone is happy".

"You are really something else, Maddie Baker, you really are", Joe retorted with pride and admiration.

"I'm Gumerson now Joe. It's a long time since I have been called Baker", she laughed.

Joe slapped his hand on his forehead as he recalled something he should have realised but had never connected with before. "Of course. Madeleine Gumerson. Frank Gumerson. I used to do your accounts for your businesses. You know I worked for Brinkley and Mather. I met Frank many times. I just never realised and I should have. How many people are called Madeleine around here? It is so uncommon".

Maddie nodded. "It really is a small world isn't it? If we had only known we could all have got together. Frank would have liked you so much, and you he, I am sure. Getting back to my name though. My mother liked an old film star called Madeleine Carroll, and named me after her. She thought that she was beautiful, and that I might take after her", she chuckled as she recalled the memory. "The only person who ever called me Madeleine was Frank when he was feeling romantic and whispering sweet nothings into my ear. Those were the days". Her eyes were serious now but again only for a moment, she was always quick not to demonstrate her grief at losing him in front of others. "You know", she continued "he wasn't really poorly. He had been exceptionally tired for a couple of weeks before, which was not like him at all, but we both put it down to him going down with something like a cold. However, this certain day he came home, rather early for him, and went into the sitting room and fell straight asleep. I left him for a short while thinking that the rest would do him some good, but you know, he wasn't asleep at all, he had just died. His heart had stopped just like that. The shock was horrific.

I went into auto mode and coped until after the funeral, but then I fell apart. People had stopped 'phoning and calling as much and I didn't want to get up out of bed, or go out, and I would not take any medication. My little dog saved my life really. She used to come upstairs and get me up when she wanted to go out, and of course she had to be fed.

Anyway, Judith my daughter had asked me to go and stay at their house, but I declined because you see they are never in. They work so many hours as they are both doctors at the local hospital.

One day my daughter came, and I was, as always sitting in the chair, staring into space and she was desperate, I know that now. She told me that she had all the sympathy in the world for me but what about herself. She was grieving too. She felt that she had lost both her mother and her father, because I was not there for her. I have got to say that her words shook me rigid, they were said with such feeling and I felt so selfish and thoughtless. I pulled myself out of that self pitying mode immediately, and got up and hugged her. Of course, we both had a long cry, but it had worked. I booked an appointment for that day at the hair salon and got dressed up. My friend Bessie next door went with me to the Mall where we had a meal and shopped.

That was the start of my beginning a new life".

The two old friends had waffled on like grasshoppers, flitting from one topic to another for some little time until they were interrupted by a knock at the door. Maddie jumped up excitedly as she so obviously knew who it would be.

The door opened, and in rushed this tiny ball of fluff, eyes all aglow and a little pink tongue hanging out and showing the joyful expression of the little dog's apparent delight at coming home.

"This is Gussie Joe. My gorgeous Gussie. I know you like dogs because you always had one when you were young". Maddie laughed with the same enthusiasm as the dog.

She then motioned to the sweet faced lady entering the room. "This is Bessie, my very dear friend and neighbour". She introduced her, whilst beckoning her to come on through into the sitting room. "Bessie, this is my very old friend Joe Bullimore, and I will not tell you how long it is since we saw one another before today".

Bessie stood in the doorway, her very pleasant face beaming a smile. A very matronly lady, who looked for all the world like someone's loving grandmother. It was apparent that she had not known that Maddie was entertaining and did not wish to interfere or intrude, but she was very nice and said that she was very pleased they had met but that she could not stay because she was having to get back as her sister in law was visiting and she would see Maddie later. With that she turned and went.

After a cuddle with her mother, Gussie went over immediately to meet Joe, who encouraged the little mite affectionately and patted her for a few moments until the animal was satisfied enough to settle down on the hearthrug, sweet contentment patterned all over her lovely face.

The reading lamps switched on and Joe almost jumped from his chair with surprise at which Maddie laughed. "It's alright Joe", she said. "The lamps are all set on timers and all come on together, there are no spooks. It is just that I like to feel safe and the lights come on whether I am in or not. It deters any strangers from coming in when they think that there is someone in the house. The garage doors are on remote control so that I do not have to get out of the car to open them. The garage itself is integral so that I do not have to come back outside to get into the house. What with that, and the infra red lights and the alarm I feel quite safe as it rather isolated around here".

With that assurance she rose from the chair and proceeded to light the gas fire. The logs were soon glowing and sending their flickering flames up the chimney all dancing around the walls in some semblance of figures. She then took herself off again into the kitchen in order to make them another drink.

Joe snuggled himself down into the comfortable armchair and closed his eyes with the same sweet contentment as the dog had shown, and recapitulated on the events of the day. He could not believe his good fortune and was delighted at Maddie's offer of a job at last. He felt that if he opened his eyes it would all have gone away and he would find that it had all been just a beautiful dream.

Maddie's voice drifted down to him and broke his thoughts. He opened his eyes and it was not a dream. She stood there with the steaming coffee, well buttered scones and deep apple pies all arranged on a tray to perfection. He sipped the coffee and devoured the home baked goodies with gusto. He complimented her once again for the umpteenth time that day.

"So your daughter Judith and her husband are both doctors then. You must be very proud of them?" Joe asked with apparent keen interest.

"Yes, we were both proud of her. Although, it was all she ever wanted to do. She met Chris at University. She was a freshman and he was in his last year before graduation. We thought that when he left to work in Norfolk, that the romance would probably peter out, but of course it didn't, and when she graduated she wanted to return to Yorkshire where her roots are. He was not bothered where he lived. It is ironic though, how they both got places at our local hospital, and they both love it even if it does take up most of their time. They want to start a family but I always say that they never get together long enough for her to conceive", she joked.

"I hope they do if that is what they really want. You would make a super grandma", Joe said sincerely imagining the scenerio.

"I have a friend you know and she is Judith's godmother. She lives at the Nooks, and that is where you said that you live Joe", Maddie continued. "Well my friend is not very well. Judith was going to see her early this morning. I wondered if you just might have seen her as she said she would be going up there early, and it is such a small cul de sac, you could just have done". She looked at Joe expectantly.

Joe's eyes widened in realisation. "Was she going to Barbara Hall's? Is she tall, slim and very attractive, with a very pleasant way with her and a nice red shiny B.M.W.?" he enquired.

Maddie's eyes danced. "Yes, that is her. Then you did see her?"

"I certainly did. She said 'good morning', to us before she went in". Joe's face grimaced involuntarily at the thought of what Trudie's comments had been. 'Never done a days work in her life', he quoted to himself. Little did she know how hard this girl worked. The hateful loathing he now felt for Trudie, which was trapped inside his whole being, welled up again automatically and almost uncontrollably.

Maddie seeing the look found it hard to interpret the expression.

"She truly is a lovely young woman Maddie, you are very fortunate", he said with sincere honesty.

At this point Joe looked at his watch and felt a

compulsion to leave as he was fearful of outstaying his welcome. It had been such a dream of a day not to be spoiled by recent thoughts of Trudie, and he had no wish to spoil it by taking advantage.

He pressed the palms of his hands on his thighs and levered himself out of the chair to a standing position. He asked if he could possibly telephone for a taxi, at which Maddie protested, stating that she could take him home, but he objected, and declined saying that there was no way that he would let her go out on her own at this time of night even if she was in her car.

The taxi arrived in only a few minutes and Maddie, her eyes exuding kindness and compassion waved him off with a kiss on the cheek. She cordially invited him to visit anytime he wished, and emphasised that she would be more than happy to see him. He knew that she meant it by the absolute sincerity in her voice but purposely avoided eye contact. He wanted her to know his innermost feelings but feared the humiliation if she really guessed the truth.

It seemed no time at all before he was home, but he was unable to expunge the loathing that he felt for Trudie. He expected her to be still up and anticipating either the silent treatment, or one of her typical balling out sessions, that he had for so long had to endure. He was in for a surprise. The house was in complete darkness and he had to let himself in with his key.

The house was silent as he turned on the hall light and climbed the stairs. He slipped quietly into the bathroom and by the time he eventually climbed into his bed he had decided not to even bother to speak to her as she lay there in the other bed pretending to be asleep.

He pulled the duvet up around his shoulders and buried his head deeper into the pillow. He would be up early tomorrow, he had a great deal to look forward to.

Chapter Five

After their return from Kenya the four pals still stayed together and continued to enjoy the camaraderie that they had shared for so long. After a one week final furlough to see their families they returned to Strensall for another month to finalise their National Service before being discharged. The regime in the camp was less harsh. Permission to leave camp was relaxed, and trips into York became more frequent. It was at this time that the four friends became blatantly aware that their relationships were soon to be drastically changed.

Barry had already begun to redesign his life, albeit unintentionally, because much as they had all been resigned to having no serious relationships with the girls they had all met, he had inadvertently drifted into a pen pal correspondence. A romantic writing relationship with Trish, whom he had met in York before they had gone to Germany. The letters had been received by Barry and secreted away from the other three for fear of reprimand because of all their initial intentions. It was not until the rest of them heard Jean Metcalfe and Cliff Michelmore reading out a request for the British Forces network on the B.B.C. Radio Light Programme, on two way Family Favourites, announcing how much she missed Barry that the boys finally realised that their buddy had been misleading them all. He had shown that he could be more than a little devious.

Barry had faced them all with some shame and trepidation, but after pretending to be disgusted with him for a short while, they all laughed and 'pulled his leg' incessantly for the remainder of the day stating that in no way were they their brother's keeper, and that they all really should be free and able to do just as they wished. The rule was only made because they had not wanted anything heavy and constricting to have to deal with whilst they were serving in the Army. Now things would be different. Girls would certainly be on the agenda and would receive top priority, so they had all set out each night for York. Barry met Trish most nights and she usually accompanied them all, but sometimes the other three would find their own amusement, whenever and wherever they could. Sometimes managing to get a little tipsy, but always remembering that they were still in the Army and not to court trouble so late in the service.

That month passed very quickly, and as the last days crept upon them, they all became more solemn, realising that this was the end of another era and much as they were all eagerly looking forward to finishing their National Service, they had all enjoyed the experience immensely. Now they would not be seeing each other again so regularly, and the realisation was very saddening.

It was Joe who came up with the bright idea that there was a way that they could all keep in contact and perhaps keep up their precious friendships for life, without any heavy promises they would not be able to keep. Every year they could all write a letter, to be duplicated three times so as to inform all of them of what had transpired that year. That way they could all be kept up to date with what each of them were doing with their lives in any given year, and occasionally they could all perhaps visit one another and meet up. After all, they were all Yorkshire lads and would be within easy reach of one another, that would be unless any of them moved which was really more than likely but in that case there would be even more reason to keep in touch by letter.

The boys were all eager to agree to the suggestion and thought it to be a splendid idea. It was decided, but it was with heavy hearts and voices trembling with natural feelings and emotions, that they all said their final goodbyes to each other on that very cold February day in 1955.

……………………........

The years had kept passing and all the men had acted true to their word. Letters had continued to pass between the four of them every February of every year and Joe felt some comfort in still being in touch and was thoroughly grateful for their true friendships. All the men had gone on to lead completely different lives to what they had imagined before they had all gone into the armed forces. All of them had always much to say in their letters and Joe was always eager in anticipation of receiving news from them. He likewise wrote much in his letters but nothing he seemed to say to them held the same excitement as they appeared to be enjoying. Well it couldn't. There was hardly ever anything of interest to tell them.

Barry and Trish had continued to see one another and by the end of the year after leaving the Army they were married. Trish was pregnant and Barry had been promoted from bus conductor at his the local bus company to Inspector of Public Transport in the York area. They had managed to rent a small terrace house, not far away from her parents house in Clifton, York.

After producing another three children in quick succession, he had been offered another promotion to

Transport Manager for Public Transportation, but in order to accept the promotion they had all had to emigrate to Perth, Australia and had all been extremely excited at the prospect of a new life out there.

Photographs were always included in the yearly letters, and every year the family appeared to grow and prosper. Barry was a happy man and looked it on every photograph and by the words in his letters. He had made the right choices in every way and was a very lucky man.

Joe had, inadvertently, been the instigator of Frank and Ron meeting their future spouses.

A few months after they had all been discharged from the forces, Joe's parents had gone away on holiday. The four buddies had a reunion and all stayed at Joe's house. The weekend had been good and had included a dance at the local Town Hall. Ted Heath and his band had been booked and everyone was thrilled at the prospect of dancing to such a wonderful orchestra, with his famous vocalists, all singing the latest ballads.

A crowd of Joe's friends were all milling around him and all eager to be introduced to his friends. Barry had brought Trish with him and so dare not show any undue interest in any of the other girls, not that he would want to, but the other two and indeed, Joe himself, were all fancy free.

They all changed partners many times but two of Joe's old playmates were showing more than a slight interest in Frank and Ron. The boys seemed to reciprocate appreciatively, so much so, that by the end of the evening Frank was smooching with Mollie and Ron was doing likewise with Brenda, to the strains of 'Cherry pink and Apple Blossom White', being played magnificently by the orchestra.

Joe had met all the girls before, he knew them all well.

There did not appear to be any fresh challenges, and so he contented himself dancing with his old friend Keith's little sister Susan, who did not appear to be his 'little' sister any longer, but some lovely swan. Nevertheless, she was taboo as far as Joe was concerned. Too young and too near in relationship to his best friend.

Fortunately for all the lads, the girls all lived in close proximity to one another. The dance had ended and they had all walked as a group depositing each girl safely home in their turn, but with a firm agreement and understanding, to all meet up the following day in the local Ice Cream Parlour, which was renowned for its delicious product.

The following day had been one of fun and laughter, all meeting on the Sunday afternoon as they had arranged the night before. Once the ice cream had been devoured, they all walked around the local park, finishing off at the 'Grecian' coffee bar beside the local bus station, to play on the juke box until it was time for the lads to catch their buses for home.

Addresses had been exchanged. Promises had been made to keep in touch, but little did any of them realise at that time that they really would.

....

By the time they all received their wedding invitations from Barry and Trish to attend their nuptials, in November that year, both Frank and Ron had bought engagement rings for Mollie and Brenda and so that day there was much to celebrate.

Only Joe remained as the one without any serious relationship, but he was by this time ensconced in the establishment of the London School of Economics, which he had decided to do in the summer and had been accepted post National Service. It was something that he wished he had done pre National Service, but had not been able to make up his mind about at that time, even though he was being well advised by his parents. He had thought at that time their advice was interference and had ignored it.

Nevertheless, he had thought well about it since his discharge and decided that it was now or never and felt sure that he had made the correct decision. He was enjoying every moment of being there, even though it was early days and he still had much to learn.

Joe was determined to put his mind to the fact that he would be studying for the next two years and with the loss of his two years in the Army he decided that it would be quite some time before he would be able to settle down financially, and he accustomed himself to that daunting fact, and accepted that it would be worth the effort eventually.

His time at university had not been wasted. He had studied hard as he had intended and made more good friends. He had enjoyed a good social life exploring the interesting public houses in the City and along the Thames. London had so much to offer in every way which was as well because the University had no campus where students could gather and so they had all to find other places where they could meet and were not short on venues.

The two years went speedily by and Joe graduated with an honours degree in mathematics and accountancy. He had acquired his 'Articles', and was now a fully qualified Chartered Accountant much to his parents obvious delight as they were now satisfied that he had not wasted his potential. Joe had returned home again to Yorkshire with the intention of working, buying his own house and settling down at last.

The four old Army comrades half expected earlier to be called back for service into the Forces when President Nasser had started a rumpus in the Suez region of Egypt. Hearts were heavy at the prospect but the call up had never materialised when the whole problem was solved at the final hour. The relief they all felt was indescribable as they had all had to put their lives on hold until the whole issue was over with.

……………………........

By the year 1958, Joe was still living at his parents house and still unattached romantically, but Frank and Mollie and Ron and Brenda were all married and house owners.

They had all had a couple of years head start on Joe but he was not downhearted or disillusioned. He had a good job with superb prospects and had his eye on a perfectly adorable girl. Her name was Leah Blackwood.

He had taken her out on several occasions and she enjoyed and shared all of Joe's interests and he hers, but she was five years younger and still had almost two years studying to complete her teachers training course at Bingley College.

She had given the impression to Joe that she was more than a little interested in him but wanted no commitments until after her training was completed, which he could appreciate and identify with, due to his own previous experience.

He had agreed that they would stay on a friendly basis and not make any real decisions about their future until some later date, and he was satisfied. There was no rush anyway.

Ron and Frank had both written as usual in the February. Both equally excited because their plan to return to Kenya and join the Police Force there had materialised.

They had both been accepted and were due to take up their posts the following June. Meanwhile, they had plenty to do in selling their newly bought houses and arranging for their furniture to be dispatched and transported to Africa before they left, in order that it could be delivered before their arrival.

Joe was elated for them as he knew that the decision to try and return there had been made whilst they were serving in that country, but little did any of them realise that their plan would materialise and come to fruition so quickly and succeed.

Of course, they must all get together again before their departure, that went without saying. Any excuse to see one another, normally, but this was something else. Another phase. Another adventure. A promise of a successful future but with an option of returning home in two years time if they could not settle or anything went wrong.

Joe admired them for their sense of adventure and nerve, but he did not envy them going to live abroad. His feet were firmly planted in Britain. He would make do with holidays and trips abroad and he would enjoy them but only if he could return home again.

Keith and Joe still continued to see one another on a regular basis, although Keith had also joined the Police Force as had always been his intention. He was courting Sally very seriously, but he was still very ambitious about his future career.

His peculiar, unsociable working hours, and his romantic life made it quite difficult for him and Joe to organise seeing one another on exact days of the week, but they managed to manipulate their lives in order to meet up quite regularly and Sally was always understanding and not one bit possessive. She made no objections at all, and so their friendship continued, still having a very special bond that they both knew they would always have and never lose.

It was at the Police Ball, where he had gone with Keith and Sally, that Joe was introduced to one of Sally's colleagues. Her name was Trudie Logan and she and Sally were both beauty consultants at a very famous Salon in Leeds. She was stunningly beautiful. She was very sophisticated with a definite air of haughtiness in her stance and never a glimmer of a smile as though she thought that she might crack her immaculately applied face make up. So absolutely different from Sally who had a natural loveliness.

Nevertheless, she was well noticed by all around her. Her appearance was so different to all the other girls and women in the dance hall.

She had been invited to the dance by Sally, not particularly as a partner for Joe but he naturally thought it would be impolite to ignore her and felt obliged to dance and converse with her for the rest of the evening. She did, however, accept many other offers besides, much to Joe's relief, but even so by the end of the evening they all four inevitably ended up together in the same car.

She was certainly extremely attractive and many men would have been delighted to have been seen out and about with her, but her personality did leave a lot to be desired and her conversation was almost non existent. He would not be asking her out again and the realisation of that fact was evident on her face as they said their goodnights on delivering her safely home. She appeared to be most displeased and walked off into the house stiff necked and indignant. She was evidently not used to being snubbed and was unable to hide the fact.

Sally had been extremely uncomfortable the rest of the way home that night and apologised profusely for having inflicted Trudie onto Joe. That had apparently, not been her intention. She explained that Trudie had been going out with someone for quite some time and he had recently ended the relationship leaving her very distressed. Sally had thought that it would be quite nice if she invited her to come to the dance. It was a nice kind gesture, which had fallen a little askew in that Trudie appeared to have taken it for granted that Joe would be asking her out and had shown contempt for him because he hadn't, which had left poor Sally feeling very embarrassed to say the least.

Joe soon put her at ease and smiled as he dropped them both off at Sally's parents house where Keith would be staying overnight, and with a promise to see them again soon.

It was almost three weeks after that dance when Joe's secretary telephoned through to him and advised him that there was a personal call for him from a young lady and should she transfer it to his office?

His face beamed. "Leah!" he thought, his heart warming, she must be coming home this weekend, something to look forward to.

Isabella put the call through to him and he answered gleefully. "Leah!" he began and then his voice trailed off in shock.

"Er, no it's Trudie", the voice murmured quietly.

"Trudie?"Joe repeated in rather a silly manner.

"Yes. I do hope that you don't mind me calling you, but Sally had mentioned where you worked and this was the only way that I knew of to contact you", she continued.

Joe was puzzled. Why would she wish to contact him when she had been so obviously rebuffed by him on that first meeting?

"I know that you might have thought that you would probably never see me again, but I am in, what one would

84

call 'a funny position' and need a favour....I don't want you to feel that you are under any obligation but I am needing a male partner to take me to a very important party on Saturday. You were the only person I knew of who could possibly take me".

There was an obvious silence for a few seconds before Joe answered. "I am the only person you knew?" he asked lamely, wondering at the lack of candidates available to her. His immediate reaction was to be at a loss for something to say. He did not wish to upset her again by refusing point blank.

"Yes, I don't know if Sally told you but I have been going out with someone for quite some time and now our relationship has finished and most of the people I know are going out with someone already. I am a bit of a loose cannon at the moment. I..I wouldn't be asking any more favours from you but you see the party I have been invited to is one for my former fiance. We are still friendly, and to be truthful I would like to be there as I am hoping that we could possibly try to reconcile, and this is the only way of I know how. A kind of last resort, don't you see?"

Joe's face brightened up now realising that his services were just a means to an end, he felt justified in accepting her invitation and doing her a favour. He readily agreed and she appeared to be elated.

They had arranged that he should pick her up from her parents house by seven o'clock the following Saturday. It was to be a bit of a 'posh do', evening suits and cocktail dresses, champagne flowing and a multi course dinner. He was not anticipating doing anything else that weekend and had nothing planned and so what had he to lose?

……………………........

He had spent most of that Saturday afternoon cleaning and

polishing his shiny new black Morris Thousand car. He valeted the inside until it was almost in mint condition and fit for a Queen.

He collected her promptly at the arranged time and she glided out of the house and down the steps looking like a million dollars in a black water mark taffeta dress with a cowl neckline, where nestled a pale pink rose, strategically positioned in the centre and complemented by sparkling black backless stiletto heeled shoes. A smart mohair stole around her shoulders and a matching clutch bag in her hand. Her raven black hair was coiffure style showing extreme sophistication with little sterling silver charms placed demurely here and there between each fold of her hair, that was the only jewellery on her person and like the last time they had met, her facial makeup was immaculate.

Joe wondered why her fiance had finished the relationship. It was certainly not because she held no physical attraction, but that was nothing to do with him at all, and so he shrugged the thought off altogether and gently escorted her into the car.

As she sat beside him on their journey to Leeds, she said very little at all but had the bloom of anticipation and expectation emanating from her, and he guessed that this party tonight was going to be an exceptionally important opportunity for her.

He pulled up and parked his car on the roadside beside Bakowski's restaurant. The pavement was already busy with guests all chattering and discussing how wonderful it was that Trevor Watson had graduated and was now a fully qualified Veterinary Surgeon at last, and that they could all celebrate his success and achievements in this way and how proud his parents were of him.

Trudie had said previously that Trevor's parents were very fond of her, and had insisted that she be invited to the

86

party as after all she had been going out with him all the duration of his University studies and should be included in the celebrations.

On entering the restaurant Joe noticed that many people acknowledged Trudie but only politely. No one gushed or held proper conversation with her, only courtesies and small talk were exchanged, but, the music was playing and everybody was seated ready for dinner almost immediately.

Even at the party, conversation between Trudie and Joe was spasmodic as she appeared to be preoccupied most of the time. Joe noticed that her face bore an expression of anger when she spotted her former fiance with another girl at the other end of the room. She was incapable of being able to conceal her displeasure, and Joe was uneasy that the other guests were noting this also. Not that it really had anything to do with him anyway, he would just try to enjoy the meal and enjoy the evening and then that, hopefully, would be that.

The meal was delightful. Joe found himself held mostly in conversation with a fat lady sitting opposite and an older man at his side, who were both very comical and pleasant and were discreetly asking no questions about his relationship with Trudie, which he was pleased about as he could not in all honesty have thought of the right and proper thing to say. He could hardly have related to them the real reason why he was there, but hoped upon hope that his selfless favour would at least bear some fruit at the end of the day, but after seeing Trevor Watson with the girl at his side he had very real doubts.

After some short but adequate speeches and a few 'Hurray Charlies' the tables were swiftly moved back and the dance floor uncovered. A small orchestra started playing the more popular dance tunes and soon everyone were whirling about on the floor.

Joe had a couple of dances with Trudie, but noticed particularly that Trevor never looked directly at her once whilst he was aware of it, which he thought was strange to say the least, when they were supposed to still be on amicable terms.

Trudie, did however, sidle up to Trevor's mother and engage her in conversation, the lady smiling rather falsely and looking somewhat ill at ease at the situation, which made it look to others that Trudie had placed her in an awkward predicament.

Joe had pretended not to notice but wondered if Trudie had been exactly truthful when she had said that the family were still on friendly terms with her. He felt that she had not realised their feelings for her or had not wanted to accept the fact.

Joe had turned to speak to the older man again and when he turned back Trudie had disappeared. He searched the room with his eyes but could not see her and pacified himself with the thought that maybe she had gone to the powder room. If she had, then she was taking a long time about it because it was a full half an hour later that a strange girl came up to him with a message from Trudie saying that he had to meet her outside where she would be waiting.

He immediately left and found her at the bottom of the restaurant stairs in obvious distress and stating profoundly that she must go home, she could not stay. She was too distressed to explain and Joe felt that he had no right to pressure her. After collecting his outdoor clothes from the cloakroom they quickly walked down the road to the car, and got in quickly driving away leaving Joe absolutely bewildered.

Trudie had sobbed uncontrollably with what Joe

thought appeared to be frustration and humiliation all the way home. He had felt awkward. He had never experienced the 'damsel in distress' phenomena before, and was quite unable to deal with it. When he asked if he could help at all the only thing she said was that never in her life would she ever let a man upset her again. The statement was made with so much venom and bitterness in her quivering voice that Joe visibly shuddered. Even so, he could not help feeling some pity for her as she had had such high hopes when they had started out but he would not have dared show any sympathy towards her at that moment for fear of reproach. She was not at all in the mood for any kind of tender words of support.

They drew up outside Trudie's home and Joe offered to take her to the door but she took him by surprise and asked him in. He declined as he had never met her parents and did not want them to get any false ideas, and anyway, how was she going to explain the state she was in in front of him?

"My parents are away", she said flatly. "They went abroad today for the week and to be quite honest I would like you to stay with me for while until I have calmed down as I don't wish to be on my own at this moment. Anyway, I feel that I owe you some kind of an explanation". Trudie whimpered now, her eyes beseeching him to concur.

Joe sighed deeply, he had no urge to hear her explanation but the night was not yet over. "In for a penny, in for a pound", he quoted wearily as he followed her into the house and closed the door.

……………………….........

As soon as he had closed the door on his way out of the

house and walked down the steps to continue down the path from Trudie's house that night, Joe felt instinctively that he would regret this night for the rest of his life. He looked at his watch, it was one a.m., and he had been in the house for a full two hours and he should have left immediately.

He had tried to pacify her as she related the reasons for her distress to him, and between the crying and the sobbing, she insisted on telling him that Trevor's mother had advised her not pursue any further relationship with her son, as it would be futile. He did not love her any more and was adamant that their previous liaison was well and truly over. He had now resumed a relationship with a former girlfriend and their intentions were very serious. They intended to announce their engagement at the end of the year and intended to marry the following year, after he had become established in his Veterinarian practice.

Trudie, had apparently not believed her. She had not wanted to accept it, and had been enraged and humiliated by her interference but had managed to arrange to meet with Trevor in an adjoining room to have his mother's statement confirmed or denied. His confirmation had apparently been brief and abrupt and because Trudie had started to berate him and cause some fuss over the issue, she had been asked to leave the party and not to ever contact him again.

Apparently, there had never been a chance of an amicable parting between him, and indeed, his family, and any hope of one in the future was well and truly over.

Apparently she had been asked to the party as a courtesy in the hope that she would at last understand her position with the family, and accept the fact that the decision had been made, and that they were all moving on without her in their lives, in the hope that she would do likewise.

Joe had listened with a sympathetic ear wondering with interest what exactly had caused the rift in the first place, but Trudie had wanted physical comfort that night and had entwined her arms around him. He had not pushed her away. He should have but he did not and his self control succumbed to temptation.

He was angry with himself. Chastising himself as he walked away from the house. He had taken advantage of her vulnerability for the sake of sexual desire, love or making love did not come into the equation.

He had never had any intention of seeing her again in the first place, and even after the events of that night, when he had taken advantage of her emotional state, he had no desire to ever contact her again, but he had lost some of his self respect and felt a complete cad.

……………………........

For the next three weeks he never saw or heard of Trudie Logan. There had been no comments on that issue from either Keith or Sally, and Joe was not sure whether Trudie had kept the facts of that night to herself, or that Keith and Sally were being especially diplomatic by not mentioning it. Joe was not one for lauding his conquests with anyone, let alone discussing that night with anyone at all, which is one that he especially wanted to forget for all time.

That particular Thursday night, he had arranged to meet up with Keith for a couple of pints and a game of darts before Keith had to go on night duty. He rose from his desk and turned to place some files on the broad window sill which served as a desk extension. He automatically glanced through the window. She was there. Trudie. Standing on the pavement outside the office. Joe had felt his face grimace instantly. He cursed under his breath and considered leaving by the rear exit of the building to avoid her.

He really did not want to see her again at all. He argued with himself for a couple of seconds and tried to reason as to why she should want to see him. He had given her no encouragement and even though she had been so upset when he last saw her he had made it quite plain that they would not be meeting again.

He picked up his fountain pen and threaded it into his top pocket, grabbed his coat from the stand and closed the door behind him, tripping down the stairs swiftly so as to get the matter over with once and for all. He had to instil upon her once again that it really would be no use at all her contacting him in the future as they really had nothing in common.

"Hello, Trudie. This is a surprise", he addressed her quietly.

She turned and raised her precisely trimmed eyebrows. "I really had no intention of contacting you again, Joe, but I really do need to speak to you about an urgent matter", she whispered her voice trembling with apparent nervousness.

"Well, I am on my way home and have an early appointment, and so it is not really a very convenient time", he answered a little curtly. He hoped that she would get the message and leave him alone. He was in no mood for any of her little talks. He concluded that what she needed was a counsellor or a good girlfriend to talk to, he thought. He was certainly no agony aunt.

"I promise that I will not keep you very long Joe, but this is very important". She was very insistent now. Her eyes widening with determination and it was obvious that she was not going to be put off lightly. She was going to have her say.

Joe motioned to the car park and directed her towards the car, opening the doors without saying a word and trying to hide his displeasure at her being there at all.

He sat and placed his right hand on the steering wheel and tapped showing his impatience at her intrusion, which was against his nature, as he was well known for his tolerance and patience. Even he had his limits and she had stretched those limits and had to recognise that he was now at the end of his tether with her. She had to get the message finally and for good.

He could see from the corner of his eye as he turned on the ignition with the intention of driving her home and listening to what she had say at the same time, so as not to waste any more time that she was curling her fingers nervously around her handkerchief. He turned to face her for a second wondering what she could possibly be so agitated about and then reversed, turned, and drove out of the car park.

"Whatever you have to say Trudie, can't concern me, can it? Haven't you got a friend, or your mother you can talk to? Surely you cannot think that I, who am almost a stranger to you can solve your problems?" Joe bit his tongue realising that his manner was a little insensitive and felt rather ashamed but nevertheless he had to instil into her that he was not interested in having anything to do with her again.

"If it's about that night Trudie, I am sorry. I really do apologise but we both of us got carried away in the circumstances. I am sure that you regret it just as much as I do, but you do appreciate that there really is no future for us together, don't you?" he continued, trying again to fathom the reason why she needed to talk to him again.

She appeared to prickle at his condescending attitude

and said rather loudly and with some sting in her voice, rasping now with anger. "That, I am afraid Joe, is up for discussion", she retorted quickly and bitterly. "There is no easy way to say this, but I must. I'm pregnant!" She thumped both her fists on her thighs as though to state that 'there I have said it!' and then slowly turned her face to meet his. Her eyes were hard and cold as steel as she watched as he braked to a standstill in complete shock.

He felt the breath leave his lungs and his eyes started to swim. Darkness started to envelop him until he gained control and then he turned, slowly to meet her eyes again.

They were still the same, only now with a kind of smug triumphant expression never to be forgotten. She was a creature of many colours, like a chameleon, who could turn her emotions and moods off and on at will, to suit her immediate intentions. He was lost. Speechless and dismayed and needing time to regain some kind of composure before he could answer her again.

His mind started whirling, grasshopper like and recapitulating on the events of that night and trying its best to make some real sense of it all, and all the time Trudie remained aloof and silent, waiting for his next agitated comments and clearly by now showing some impatience and allowing him no leeway for the shock information she had just showered upon him.

He licked his lips and tried to swallow, his mouth now very dry and perspiration bursting from his brow. "You can't be. It's impossible!" he burst out almost angrily, thinking what a silly woman she was to even think it.

"Of course it's not impossible and I AM", she retorted back, her throat croaking now and her nose twitching with fury at being contradicted. "You don't think that I would lie about such a thing, do you?"

Joe had winced, she had not been willing to give him

credit for being so shocked, and astounded at her announcement and he had sat there once again, grey faced and ragged and feeling as cold as if he had just stepped into an ice box, even though he was still sweating profusely with a kind of fear he had never experienced before.

She continued now as though she was enjoying witnessing his discomfort. "You never used any kind of contraceptive and so, of course, I could be pregnant". She stopped again as though she was trying to imagine what he was thinking.

Joe snapped back at her, showing how cross he was. "I have hardly ever used anything before, but I never got anyone pregnant before either", he said with some indignation at her preposterous suggestion. " Men do not always go out with the intention of having sex. I am hardly ever prepared, but I have always been considerate and careful, as I was with you. If had thought for one moment that I could have been careless, I would have admitted it, not tried to deny it. I would have accepted my responsibilities without any argument".

"Am I going to have an argument Joe?" She purred sarcastically with a little girl lost voice, that annoyed Joe even more than her brusque and natural stiffness. This woman could certainly act.

Quickly, Joe sat himself upright from the slouching position he had sunk into in his dismay and asserted himself. "Not tonight Trudie, you're not. I am taking you home and going home myself to have a good long think about the issue. I will contact you myself in a few days and arrange to meet. Meanwhile, you will have to bring me positive proof of your pregnancy, before I will even discuss the matter with you again. You have got to understand that this has all been a terrific shock to me and so naturally, I cannot go into this lightly, nor can I make any commitments of any kind at this stage. My God! I have only known you vaguely for a few hours in my life, what a nightmare!"

Trudie stared forward and elicited no response this time, apart from a sigh of indignation. This was a disaster, nevertheless, there would be nothing to prevent this drama of the future from unfolding pretty soon Joe was sure. Everyone would be aware of it. He clenched his teeth. The muscles in his jaws contracted as he cringed at the thought of how he was to solve this catastrophe. What would eventually be the outcome?

…………………………........

Keith's mouth visually sagged. His eyes drooped and Joe felt that even his beloved friend's ears would have flopped had they been long enough. He related his story to him that night. His pallor reflected that of Joe's own. Grey-white with absolute shock as he stared back at him in disbelief.

As the story enfolded in all its entirety, leaving nothing out at all, Keith's astonishment never once diminished as he held on to every word. Joe was grateful for his friend's sincere and sympathetic ear but was, at the same time, praying that he could come up with some kind of miracle to obliterate the facts and memories from his tired mind. Tell him he had been dreaming and that it was all a very nasty nightmare from which he would awaken at any moment. Instead, Keith remained true to himself and after offering Joe his heartfelt commiserations proceeded to offer good advice and some proposals on such a delicate matter for Joe to consider.

"Well, the first thing Joe that I know you will have

considered, is marrying the girl, but you can't do that when you don't really know her. Not yet at any rate. If I know you, which I think I do, you would not want some other man bringing up your child, and you would not be suggesting that she have the child adopted, because that way you would most probably never see the child again. Abortion is not legal, and I don't think that would be an option for you anyway. The only thing that I can suggest is that you start seeing her on a regular basis to see if you can get along and make a 'go' of things. If you can't then make your decision then. There really is nothing that I can say that you haven't thought of yourself and there really is no reason to make that decision right now, today. Good heavens Joe, you are still in shock, don't do anything too hastily".

Their conversation, until Keith had to leave for work, continued on in mostly the same vein, recapitulating over and over again on the same proposals, their minds doing mental leapfrogs until they were weary of the repetition.

They were both in agreement that Joe would have to accept the inevitable truth. Accept the concept of future fatherhood and try to redesign his life, albeit, however reluctantly.

He would have to appeal to Trudie's better nature and insist that she be patient and take everything day by day until they had had time to come to some real decisions, that would be beneficial to both of them, however long it took.

It all sounded so simple in theory, but it was not going to be. Their parents would be to tell. Their reputations would be scarred. There would be embarrassments and humiliations to contend with. He wished that he had a skin like a rhinoceros. He must have a brain like one he thought because otherwise, he would not have been in this position in the first place, and why he was, was still a complete enigma.

…………………….......

Joe had scanned the faces of his parents intently, as he carefully explained his predicament in great detail omitting nothing. He was making no excuses for himself. He couldn't. He would have to accept the responsibility for his foolish actions one way or another. He did, however, attempt to apologise for letting them down and showed sincere remorse for any embarrassment that this might cause them.

They both remained silent for the duration of his story, never interrupting once. Their faces and body language could easily be interpreted and Joe realised their expressions showed mixtures of shock, with which he could identify. They both emanated disappointment and great sadness, their emotions so strong that he could feel them both reaching out to him.

He had gained real comfort from this. There was going to be no reproaches, no chastising, nothing negative. The deed was done and could not be undone. There could be no looking back and no 'if only', after all their son was a grown and experienced man.

His predicament was again discussed in great detail in much the same vein for the next couple of hours. Some positive suggestions were made, but at the end of the day both Celia and Bob had come to the same conclusion. They knew he would remain level headed and make the right decision in the end and whatever he chose to do he could rely on them wholeheartedly for their total support. Joe had been delighted at their response, although not totally surprised.

Trudie's parents were a different proposition. He had never met them. He knew absolutely nothing about them. He had no idea what to expect. He did not know anyone who knew them, who could enlighten him. Trudie never really mentioned them at all, which was no surprise.

He was going forward into the unknown and was quite in awe of the fact that he would be going in blind and would have to prepare in advance.

Chapter Six

Perhaps one of the very worst parts of Joe's trauma was having to contact Leah. He could not bear to think that he would have to hurt her and was not willing to wait for her to come home from college and perhaps hear the news second hand. He owed her that much, and so he wrote to her, just a short note asking her if it would be possible for him to meet her at their usual meeting place. The Whistler Public House in Bingley, and that he would explain when he saw her.

Leah responded with alacrity, obviously wondering what could be so very important or urgent that he was not able to see her and tell her at the weekend.

Joe had arrived there early and she was prompt as ever. He ordered the drinks and a bar snack and then sat down and immediately took her hand in his and looked deeply into her eyes. His face was by now showing distinct signs of complete weariness and hopelessness. He knew that he would not have to dither whilst explaining his predicament to her, he would have to be explicit no matter how cruel it seemed. He could not attempt to expiate or exonerate himself to her. Facts were facts, and once the sad and tragic story was told, he did not expect any sympathy or forgiveness only an angry or tearful response. He was in for some surprise because not only was she not cross or emotional in any way but quite the opposite.

"You know, Joe," Leah whispered, quietly, so that the

other customers could not overhear their conversation, "you really do not have to explain, or apologise to me so reverently. We love each other I know, but we were never really seriously committed. You know that, but I am so very sorry that you are in this preposterous situation. I have got to say that am really in no position to reprimand you or reproach you. I am sure that you will be in sufficient agony without me putting my 'fillings' in, so to speak."

She squeezed his hand firmly, hoping to pacify him or give him some kind of assurance or encouragement, he looked as though he needed it, he looked so ragged.

"Joe", she continued showing genuine care and sympathy on her lovely face. "We could, any of us end up in a similar predicament. We never know. One foolish act, one silly moment, a little too much to drink…", she trailed off.

Joe stood and pulled her up from her chair. He put his arms around her and hugged her, showing all the affection he felt for her and silently thanking her for not being haughty or confrontational. Her words had been kind and thoughtful, full of compassion as she must have felt the necessity to try and alleviate his embarrassment and suffering. She had succeeded more than she knew and he was extremely grateful for that.

He left her with a heavy heart knowing that there would never be a relationship of any kind between them again, only perhaps of fond friendship, never anything more intimate than that. To a certain extent he was pacified and felt more relaxed as he drove home that night.

There was, as far as he could ascertain, only one more obstacle to eliminate and he did not relish that thought.

…………………….......

Busybodies, broccoli and bananas were three of Joe's pet hates. Trudie had eventually condescended to take Joe home to meet her parents for a meal and a discussion only one week after she had shown him positive proof of her pregnancy.

She had already informed them of her pregnancy, but had not elaborated very distinctly on their response. Joe was not really sure of what he could expect, or what kind of reception he would receive, on initially meeting them.

He received a cool but polite welcome and was quickly ushered into the dining room where the meal was obviously ready to be served. No doubt they thought that things might be difficult and matters could be discussed in a more amiable and relaxed manner over a meal. Joe did not object to that at all. The more relaxed the better.

To his astonishment he felt no embarrassment or discomfort at all, which he put down to the unfamiliarity of never knowing them before, but this endowed him with a new sense of self confidence and self assurance.

The first course was broccoli soup with hot rolls and butter, the latter compensating by eliminating the taste of the soup. The main course was beef and two vegetables, one of the vegetables being broccoli and the dessert was banana split! Joe ate it all. He dared do no other. He waited to see if the busybody would appear and would deal with that if it emerged, as and when.

Bertha Logan was a sharp featured, beady eyed woman, whose chin and nose were so prominent that they almost met one another. She was as thin as a rail and grimly dressed all in black, with no accessories to alleviate the bleakness of the outfit. She smiled not at all, throughout the whole meal and spoke as infrequently. She did stare though and glared at Joe once or twice and appeared to miss nothing at all about him, from his bodily physique to the clothes he was wearing, which could have been somewhat unnerving had he allowed it to be.

William Logan on the other hand had plenty to say. He was of average height with a fat bloated face, a large nose and puffy eyes which were probably the result of excessive brandy indulgence. He had a balding head and was quite portly in stature, but in his favour he was pleasant enough to talk to. He appeared to be more obsessed with his influence and social standing in the community as a local Labour Councillor than with his only daughter's predicament.

Afterwards, William expedited a constant flow of never ending questions, in quick succession, which reverberated in Joe's ears until they were ringing from the overflow. It was as though he must ask all the inevitable questions, which had more than likely been rehearsed beforehand, and must be eradicated and put out of the way as speedily as possible. "What was Joe's attitude to the matter? Was he dependable? Did he want to be seriously involved? Could he be committed sufficiently, enough to share his life with Trudie? What were his Politics? and did he believe in God?"

Joe was willing to give William the benefit of his doubts about him being a 'nosy parker', because, after all, it was he, Joe, who was the instigator of Trudie's downfall. It could only be expected that her parents would wish to discover everything about him that they possibly could. It could only be more beneficial to them but why did he get the distinct feeling that he was dealing with some kind of hierarchy, member of the Hoi Polloi? Did they think of him as some kind of ignorant moron who had no more sense than to impregnate their daughter on their first encounter in the sex stakes?

William consequently went on to elaborate on how

marriage was an obstacle course, a test of endurance, which could be a constant strain and could test your tolerance to the limits!

In all this time neither Trudie nor her mother uttered a word. There were many sighs as though they had heard it all before, but there were no objections, and Joe had guessed that they had both been warned beforehand not to butt into the conversation before he was done.

Apart from answering the questions as and when they were being fired at him, Joe said very little himself. He was willing to allow her father to stand on his soapbox until he had reached saturation point. He would say his piece, briefly and concisely, so that nothing would be left unsaid and they would both be left in no doubt what his intentions were for the future. He was in no way going to be dictated to. He would take advice if it were given unpretentiously, but they would see clearly that the decisions would be his at the end of the day.

Trudie did not come into the equation fully during the discussion. Joe had already gathered from the conversation that all she wanted, and was interested in, and aiming for was acquiring a husband. She wanted a home to give her respectability if nothing else.

By the end of the evening Bertha and William were pacified by the fact that Joe would continue taking their daughter out on a regular basis, and that if, by the end of a few months they had found some kind of compatibility they would marry. If not, then Joe would be willing to maintain the child financially and share in the child's upbringing to the best of his ability. Meanwhile, he would buy a modest house because now the time was overdue to set up home himself, and leave the comfort of his mother's nest, no matter how the situation developed with Trudie in the future. He wanted to be prepared for any event and felt that this was the best course of action to take.

After that unforgettable meeting matters were taking their course, slowly but surely. Joe felt more at ease at providing himself with several options and having laid them out with some assertiveness after finding that new confidence. But, little did he know at that time that words like 'Manipulation' and 'Intimidation', would be entering in on his cosy environment and existence, and that alien beings would be taking over his world as he knew it.

………………………........

The days passed into weeks and the weeks into months. Joe continued with his courtship of Trudie. They had very little in common as far as interests and conversational stimulation were concerned, but a least she seemed amiable enough and was doing her very best to win his affection.

Joe knew that his mother and father had been disappointed at the loss of Leah as a potential daughter in law, but nevertheless, he had eventually taken Trudie to meet his parents who never commented one way or another about how they felt about her. Joe had no intention of asking them in case he placed them in an awkward predicament. He felt that if there was anything at all they really wished to say then they would say it without any invitation from him, and so he let things be. He knew that they would be trying their hardest to come to terms with the situation in their own way.

True to his word, Joe bought a modest terrace house with three bedrooms, lounge, kitchen and bathroom. It had a tiny patch of garden at the front, but a very long one at the rear. The vendors were leaving the garden hut and all the garden tools, as they were moving into a flat and would not need them any longer themselves. There was the added bonus of a garage, and all for the fair price of £950.

The house was very nicely decorated and very clean. Joe moved into it immediately after the contract had been signed.

He could not afford very much furniture but what he did buy was of good quality. The kitchen was well furnished with washer, cooker and refrigerator and ample units fitted throughout. His mother provided him with many utensils, cooking pots, towels, table and bed linen, and now he was satisfied that whatever decision was made about Trudie the house would suffice in any way, with or without her.

Joe had never made the mistake of seeing Trudie every night. He felt that they both needed an element of 'space' to do other things, and see other people. If he did decide to marry her, then that would be the time to see more of her. He had never invited her to move in with him, even for a trial period or even hinted that she might stay overnight as that would have been catastrophic had he decided not to prolong the relationship. Sex was never on the agenda, he was committed enough as it was but she never complained or commented on the fact, she appeared to be contented enough with the arrangement.

Keith and Sally were real stalwarts, never failing in their support of either of them, which was very fair and generous of them both. They joined them on evenings out, either going to the cinema or meals out, and so it was by no means surprising when four months after Trudie's announcement of her pregnancy, Keith and Sally were standing by their sides, acting as witnesses at the local Registry office, with only Trudie and Joe's parents in attendance as they repeated their vows at their wedding.

Joe would never forget that day. It was raining hard and no one smiled. It was like a damning omen to their future. There were no other guests and only nine people in the room, including the registrar.

"I, Joe John Bullimore, take you Gertrude May Logan…" The Registrar's voice trailed on asking him to repeat her words after her and everything seemed to be a mental and visual blur. "Gertrude May!" he thought to himself. Due to the ludicrous tradition of retaining family names for posterity, adhered to by parents sometimes perhaps hoping to inherit, but more than often causing acute embarrassment to the offspring, which was so in Trudie's case as he felt her squirm at the very fact that she was bound to repeat it during the nuptials. No wonder they had shortened it and called her 'Trudie'. His own name was a bit dated but he could live with it, it did not embarrass him.

Joe was upset that things could not have been different as all his old friends were not there for him, as he had been for them. Trudie's family obviously thought that there was not a lot to celebrate and wanted as little fuss and publicity as possible.

He felt that he had no right to object at all due to the circumstances.

After the ceremony congratulations were shyly offered. Photographs were taken outside the country club just to mark the occasion, but there was no official photographer just a clever amateur associate of William's, but it suited Celia who felt that they needed some kind of reminder of the day as a token gesture.

They all enjoyed a fine wedding breakfast and Trudie had looked as immaculate as ever wearing a coffee coloured guipure lace two piece suit with bronze coloured accessories, whilst Sally wore a champagne coloured chiffon dress in contrast. Both of them very attractive young women. Trudie being as dark haired as Sally was blonde.

After the toast, Joe could only indulge in one more drink before they had to trace their way to the car park. There were hugs and kisses and well meaning comments all round as they drove off in the little Morris 1000 car. On through Bradford to Skipton and further north into the Lake District where they were to spend their few days honeymoon.

The rain never bated as they meandered through the winding country lanes and as they travelled there was not much conversation which he now accepted was the norm with his new bride. He retraced in his mind the events of the day. He remembered that before they had all departed from the house his father taking him aside and instilling into him that it was not too late to back out. He remembered how William had been well tipsy on his arrival at the Registry office and that Bertha was still wearing black and obviously in mourning for her daughter's fall from grace.

His mind alerted again when they came to Bowness on Lake Windermere. By this time the light had begun to fade. It was a happy relief to be greeted by the owner of the Inn where they would be staying and a piping hot meal was waiting for them in front of a very comforting roaring fire.

After dinner, Trudie was in very high spirits which was something that Joe had never experienced before when he had been with her and was slightly amused by her, but at the same time rather unnerved. Her cheeks were very highly flushed and her eyes exceptionally over bright. She talked and talked, recalling the events of the day in excited tones and proffering a profusion of ways that they might improve the house and garden and many other things when they returned back home. It was as though she dared not make any suggestions before they were married as she had felt that she had no real right until then.

Joe was agog with amazement. The words were cascading from her mouth like there would be no other time to discuss such things. He could hardly get a word in but assumed that she had been on tenterhooks for so long as to how their relationship would develop and how it would all finish up in the end. Now that she had actually managed to get married her emotions had reached a climax, resulting in her whole being, being capitulated into this hyper state because of her new found security and stability. A real sense of relief. Of course, it must be, there was no other explanation, she would have calmed down by morning.

Their bedroom was just as cosy and comfortable as the dining room and lounge had been. Their bed was a giant four poster and the furniture large, heavy and dark. The fire was glowing in the hearth and it was a very romantic setting. A bottle of champagne and two glass flutes stood beside a bowl of fresh fruit on a small table with a couple of comfortable easy chairs inviting them to sit and enjoy.

They undressed and bathed, privately in turn, and proceeded to get gingerly and shyly into bed.

Joe realised that she was now quite heavy with pregnancy and would be very tired after the excitement of the day. He offered only his arm to cradle her head and made no advances as to lovemaking. If she was disappointed, then he would sense it and act accordingly. She was not disappointed and seemed grateful for his consideration and soon drifted off to sleep. Joe sighed. Not even a kiss. There would be other days he assured himself.

………………………........

The honeymoon had been successful to a point. They had toured the Lakes and explored many places not seen before by either of them, and enjoyed it all. Joe had winced at the fact, that the only reference to their coming baby was made by Joe when he bought a Peter Rabbit cuddly toy from a shop, together with a book by Beatrix Potter for future bedtime stories.

By the end of the honeymoon the consummation of the marriage had still not been fulfilled, as every time he had made any advances she had rebuffed him, making excuses about her condition. He had not pursued the fact not knowing too much about the ins and outs of such things, never daring to ask his mother beforehand afraid of been likened to some ignorant wimp.

Life with Trudie settled in at their home at 10, Belvedere Terrace. She gave up working and Joe continued on in much the same vein as before. There were rituals of visiting both sets of parents and going for short drives in the car. Sometimes, but only occasionally, seeing some of their friends for nights out and other normal activities.

Trudie's housekeeping and cookery skills were faultless, but there was still no sparkle or real rapport between them, only a comfortable existence. Joe forced himself to hope that it would eventually improve. The love would come later. Ever optimistic Joe. Little did he know!

………………………........

Joe glanced at the bedside clock and noticed that the time was four a.m., he had been nudged awake by Trudie's elbow as she whispered for him to get out of bed. He turned and looked her full in the face wondering what on earth could be the matter, when full realisation hit him

"The baby?" he almost shouted asking in his still dazed state.

She nodded.

"But.. it's not time!" he almost yelled. "It's too early. Are you sure?"

"Yes, I am sure. But don't panic, there is still plenty of time", she answered quietly but purposefully. "Sometimes babies can't wait and come early, prematurely, but it could be a false alarm. We need to see a professional or someone expert to be sure, so we do need to go to the hospital to find out. Better to be safe than sorry, don't you think?"

Of course, Joe was eager to agree not wanting anything untoward to happen at this late date, and everything had been prepared beforehand. Nothing to do but get dressed and this he did with great rapidity.

Trudie, on the other hand was dressing slowly and precisely, showing no signs of nerves or stress at all. Her cool collectiveness astounded him, but he did admire her for it. It was as though she was no novice to the procedure and he felt that she did not fully comprehend the meaning of his fear for her going into premature labour, but he did not elaborate for fear of frightening her.

On reaching the maternity hospital she was admitted in a most regimental fashion, everything being handled methodically and with strict precision and then taken away to be put to bed and examined.

Joe was quickly ushered away and informed that he could either stay in the waiting room or go home as there would be nothing that he could do if he stayed, but that he was welcome to telephone periodically if he so wished.

He had stayed on for a couple of hours before he realised that he was wasting his time. He had climbed wearily into his car and driven home, worrying a little if the baby would be alright due to the premature birth.

He had refrained from asking any questions whilst he was there, as the frosty faced sister in charge appeared to be more preoccupied with getting Trudie placed comfortably than answering any of Joe's questions. Rightly so, he thought. He could understand that her well being had first priority.

He had made a decision not to telephone either parents due to the unreasonable time and had eventually fallen asleep. He awoke at eight thirty a.m., and immediately telephoned the hospital from the kiosk at the corner of the lane.

A boy. Born ten minutes ago. Both mother and infant doing well. No complications at all but the nurse not wishing to elaborate further over the telephone, but informed him that he could visit, but only for ten minutes, until the evening visiting time, when visiting would be fathers only allowed. Other visitors only at allocated times during the afternoons of weekdays and weekends.

Joe was elated. He quickly telephoned Trudie's parents and then his own, not forgetting to contact the office to let them know, and inform them, that he would not be into work today.

Within a few minutes, Joe was standing by Trudie's bedside, showing a little concern at the look of weariness on her face, but at the same time looking down at the canvas cot by the side of the bed, beaming proudly at his perfectly beautiful son.

Questions about his son's welfare poured out of his mouth. Would it be any detriment, him being born prematurely? Was he at risk in any way?

Trudie reassured him that everything was fine and not to bother any of the staff with questions, because they were busy enough as it was.

Joe was pacified for now. He did not want to be a

nuisance. His mother would know, being a District Nurse, if there was anything to fear.

And so, started a wonderful relationship between him and David, his treasured son that never ever faltered.

…………………….......

The fact that Trudie never really bonded with her son bothered Joe terribly, but apart from a few quite insignificant comments, Joe chose not to broach the subject too deeply as he always hoped and felt strongly that things would change. They never did.

She kept the child well clothed and fed, immaculately clean and took him out walking, but she never really played with him or picked him up for a cuddle or even looked at him lovingly as Joe had always been used to in his own childhood. It was a little unnerving but David never appeared to mind or miss the attention and he never commented because he had never known anything else from her.

He knew, and accepted, that any displays of affection came from his father and he appeared to be content with that but it made Joe feel sad for him as he surely felt that the loving should come from all sides and that David was missing out on a great deal.

As time wore on Joe came to accept, albeit reluctantly, that Trudie's maternal instincts were either practically nil or even non existent, but nevertheless, he decided when David was three years old that it was time to think about another child.

He had nervously approached Trudie one night in bed with the suggestion. She had immediately recoiled, as though the idea was repulsive to her. Joe was shocked at her venomous reaction. He had anticipated that he might have to talk her into the proposition but never expected such a deadly reaction. He was devastated, so much so that he knew that any further discussion on the matter would have been taboo. He was sickened at the futility of it all and more than reluctantly decided to drop any thoughts of any more children entering into their household.

Trudie never did return to work at the salon, but did travel about to different lady clients to administer her beautician skills as and when they needed to be pampered. She had learned to drive before they were married and her father had bought her an Austin Mini car which gave her a considerable element of independence. It made it possible for her to continue to buy the clothes and cosmetics that she had been accustomed to having.

Meanwhile Joe's parents continued to be supportive and loving towards their only grandchild but his maternal grandparents treated him with the same indifference and cool attitude that Trudie had always portrayed towards him.

As time went on, David proved to be a good, bright scholar and Joe always showed a very keen interest in anything that the boy did.

He was a popular boy and had many friends who Joe and his paternal grandpa often gathered together for scouting trips and other similar pastimes. The boys were all a great delight to both the men and they never tired of participating in anything the lads chose to do. They chose to do something practically every weekend. Life was exciting and a great pleasure, whether it be summer activities or winter sports. They all indulged in whatever was going on at any given time and David's friends parents were always pleased to let their offspring participate and join in all the fun.

…………………………........

Trudie had not enthused about them having to move to Nottingham but, surprisingly, she had not refused to go either. Once they had got established into their new home, she had quickly found new clientele and continued with her mobile health and beauty programme and even rented a building to be used as a venue for the same.

This seemed to have consoled her, but David missed his grandpa and his friends enormously in the beginning, which in turn made Joe feel as though they should not have moved, and he began to regret his actions. However, he need not have fretted because it was not very long before David had settled into his new school and environment and made many other friends. He had never complained but Joe had insisted that he keep in touch with his old friends in Yorkshire, even though he often wished he had not put the boy through such trauma, but he realised that children were resilient and he soon coped very well much to Joe's relief.

As the years sped on David had shown his worth academically and his standards and grades never fell. He was capable of going on to University, and Joe had made many allowances for this and had encouraged him, but David had a mind and thoughts of his own.

"The Army!?", Joe exclaimed, questioning with surprise his son's revelation that night.

"Yes, Dad. It is my ambition and intention to make it a career. I have already made an application to the Marines. I am waiting to hear from them and if they accept me then I will continue to study and qualify once in the Forces".

Joe had gulped. He had no idea that David had any such leanings. He was tall and strong in physique. Athletic and healthy and very outgoing and would be a typical candidate, but well, it was such a surprise.

David had continued grinning at his father's stunned

115

expression. "I would be leaving home no matter what, Dad, you know that". His smile broadened out knowing full well that whatever he chose to do his father would give him his full support and all the encouragement he could muster. He would never have been railroaded into anything that he did not want to do.

"Of course it's alright son, you know that. It goes without saying. It is just that I had no idea that that was your intention. You never gave any indication, that's all". He had answered reassuringly and then added, "Have you told your mother?"

"No, but I will of course. Not that she will care one way or the other, you know that Dad", David replied still smiling, but with a hint of sadness which could not be disguised or concealed by any jocular pretence about Trudie's attitude towards him.

David had always been aware of his mother's icy stance but she had never offered any tenable justification for it, and he had never asked. He was not judgemental. She must have had her reasons and he had accepted that, even though it had puzzled him and he was curious. He would really have liked to know.

Joe looked at his son with real pride and thought nostalgically about his own mother when he himself was going away into the forces and the grief she had felt as he marched down the railway station platform, her watching, unknown to Joe at the time, but laughed about afterwards.

David stood in front of him, tall and dark haired with fine features and a good stance.. He would make a fine soldier. And he did.

…………………….......

Four years later and well established in his career with

116

promotion to Officer rank, David was making plans to marry a wonderful girl called Victoria. The house was bought and the plans for the wedding were being finalised and everything was almost ready for the big day, and everyone was excited.

The telephone rang in the middle of the night. Joe picked up the receiver and answered quickly.

Victoria was explaining between sobs, a little incoherently, and eventually Joe placed the receiver back on the telephone. Trudie did not rouse, she lay there still asleep. Joe turned from the bed and placed his feet firmly on the floor cradling his chin in his cupped hands and staring, staring into complete dark nothingness for what seemed to be an eternity.

The reality would not register. David was DEAD. Killed. Special job, together with the S.A.S. unit. Infiltration of some kind in Northern Ireland…His body was to be returned tomorrow from Ulster at seventeen hundred hours. Next of kin to be notified officially. A full Regimental funeral.

The noise deafened him. What was it? Until Joe realised the thundering noise had emanated from his own sobbing which was uncontrollable and his heart beating so wildly that it almost choked him.

Trudie awoke now, showing real alarm on her usually unemotional face. Joe's lamentations turned still uncontrollably into some kind of laughing hysteria. The alarm on Trudie's face continued to escalate. She slapped him hard across his face. Frightened, as she had never before witnessed him losing his self control. He gradually calmed and dictated to her the horrific tragedy which had befallen their son.

She never gasped or murmured any kind of comment. She just sat there and stared, her dark eyes visibly glassing over as he watched intently for her reaction.

He made to put his arms around her, to comfort them both, but she pushed him away viciously and alighted from the bed like some ghostly spectre and pulled on her robe. Without looking back she started down the stairs and after a few minutes he followed, feeling that she was suffering from terrible shock.

Once downstairs his eyes widened with disbelief. The kettle was on the stove, and in her hand was the telephone receiver. She was coolly, almost callously informing her father of the tragedy. No tears. No sign of remorse but still Joe was willing to give her the benefit of doubt, thinking that she was suffering from extreme trauma and had not grasped the horrific situation in all its entirety. He was so wrong.

She never wept for her son. Her actions were as mechanical as ever. Her life at that time continued on as if nothing at all had happened. There was no consolation for him from her and she needed none at all from him or indeed anyone else. She had made that perfectly obvious from the beginning, stating that if he chose that course of career he must have known what risks he would be taking.

Bob and Celia were devastated and grieved with their son in their shared loss and the terrible fact that Trudie was so grim and relentless of her treatment of him.

William Logan did look somewhat grief stricken, but her mother remained, as always, blank.

Joe knew from that moment that he would always grieve for David and the pain was so intense so as to make it unbearable and that now his life was about to change again forever.

……………………........

Lovemaking had never existed between Joe and Trudie

and sex had been very slow to start and afterwards always been spasmodic. A marital duty to be suffered by Trudie who was always icily frigid leaving Joe feeling that he had ultimately raped her in some kind of way.

After David's funeral, their double bed was replaced by twin beds, albeit in the same room, but sex of any kind became extinct and even talk of it was strictly taboo.

Joe never even contemplated any discussion on the matter anyway. The idea of sleeping with or making advances to Trudie was just as abhorrent to him as he imagined it was to her. He knew that she secretly reviled him. He could identify with that feeling as he shared it.

…………………….......

Erin and Max Anderson were colleagues and friends. Max shared senior accountancy status with Joe and Erin was the company secretary for the firm. Joe spent many nights of enjoyment down at the local pub with Max, who unfortunately for Erin had a roving eye for the ladies, which was a great pity because Erin was so obviously in love with him.

Joe had found himself back at their house for a late night take away supper after they had left the local and Erin was always glad to see him socially. It was a well known fact at the office that things were drastically wrong with Joe's marriage, even though it was never discussed by him. People had come to their own conclusions and he was never questioned and nothing was ever said.

Erin liked Joe. His dry wit and sense of humour and they all enjoyed social outings but could only participate spasmodically due to the fact that they had a son, Miles, and no regular child minder, except of course for the one that he went to daily whilst his mother worked. Erin was trying to juggle a full time career and bring up her son, but she was, unlike Trudie, a wonderful mother and her son always took first priority over going out socially. She always felt that she spent enough time away from the child when she was at work and would not leave him regularly to pursue social activities without him.

Joe's relationship with the Andersons had lasted for about two years, until one morning Max was late for work. Erin had crept into the office stealthily and silently, obviously hoping not to be noticed, but her efforts were in vain as everyone did, if only for the fact that she was quiet which was very unusual for her. She usually breezed in like a breath of spring air. On closer look it was plain to see that she had been crying profusely as her eyes were red and puffy. Anyone else would probably have telephoned in sick, but not Erin, always conscientious to the last.

Everyone being very discreet as always, never asked her what the matter was. She would say herself if she had wanted anyone to know. Joe was no different, he kept his counsel, although he was extremely concerned for her and wished that he could erase the misery she must be feeling.

Max never came to work that day. Nor the next few days. There was still no explanation from Erin as to what the problem was, even though she continued to be in work on time each day and carried on being as industrious as ever.

Almost a week had passed and still no word from Max or explanation from Erin. Joe stood up from his desk and pulled on his coat. It was lunchtime and he always went to the Black Bull, in the square opposite the office, for his lunch. He closed the office door behind him and started towards the stairs. Erin was climbing back to the office with a polystyrene carton in her hand containing a jacket potato with cheese filling. Joe could smell it from halfway up the stairs.

She looked up and smiled at him. A genuine smile but with sad almost tragic eyes looking straight into his.

"You are not having that Erin, you need a proper meal", Joe cried out with concern, knowing full well that this would probably be the only meal she would have that day. He continued, "I am going to bully you into coming over to the 'Bull' with me to have something more substantial", he said as he tried to be jovial and put her at her ease.

She made to protest at first and then thought better of it and succumbed, feeling that she needed an outlet for her pain and misery. Joe was the only person that she could trust with the information she was about to divulge. After all, he had a right to know, as a colleague, but more so as a dear friend and he had not attempted to pry in any way, and even now had not asked any questions. Joe was relieved that she had not objected to going with him and he took the carton from her hand and placed it on her desk. Together, they descended down the stairs and across the road.

Fortunately, there was a two seat booth at the rear of the 'Bull' and they quickly grabbed it and were seated before anyone else had the same thoughts. Joe ordered their meal at the bar and quickly returned to sit with her taking two glasses of medium white wine along with him.

Sitting opposite her he said nothing at first, only looking her full in the face and then placing his hands on hers on the table as a gesture of sympathy. He hoped that she would respond and open up and verbally bare all her troubles to his caring ears.

Her eyes were damp and she lowered her head in embarrassment.

"Max has left me Joe", she whispered softly and without looking up. "He's gone to Canada. He says that he needs some space, away from Miles and me. He says that he feels suffocated and trapped and needs time to think and so needs to take a sabbatical whilst he sorts himself out. I don't know what to do. I am so tired of thinking. All I want to do is sleep. I feel so depressed and Miles is asking for explanations. What am I to tell him Joe? Daddy doesn't want us? I can't say that to him".

Erin's voice continued to quiver. She was using all her self control to stop herself from crying out loud. Her hand was fisted with utter frustration as she thumped it on the table as silently as she could showing her anger and sorrow. Using all the power that she could muster not to make a spectacle of herself.

Joe was sickened by the news but not altogether surprised. He had always known that Max had never been able to fully control his wanderlust in any department, neither with women nor in the dream stakes, which was really a great pity because he had a fine brain and a wonderful life with Erin and Miles, but it was obviously not enough for him.

"Perhaps it is just like he says Erin. He might just want some time on his own to gather his thoughts and decide what he really wants from life", Joe tried to console her. "He may eventually come to the conclusion that the grass is no greener wherever he is and decide that he had made a grave mistake".

Erin did not appear to be pacified. He wondered if he might have said the wrong thing by planting seeds of hope into her mind. What if he never came back to her? What if after a while she did not want him back?

She fiddled about with her fingers absently turning her glass this way and that. Suddenly, she brought the glass up to her mouth and downed the lot in one gulp,

"I need something stronger. Get me a double gin and

tonic Joe, please. To hell with him. Who cares anyway?" She looked up at him smiling a little idiotically he thought, and he stared in disbelief back at her. She was obviously so distraught as to be verging on hysteria and he could identify with that emotion at times of real stress.

"Come on Erin. I'm going to take you home and I am going to stay with you until you have calmed down", Joe said faking a masterful attitude.

"Not until I have another drink", she replied defiantly.

"I will make you a drink when you get home", he said defying her. "But only one. You are not going to sink your sorrows in a bottle, that really is the wrong way to deal with this and you have Miles to think about".

She dutifully raised herself from the bench and followed him out of the pub, him apologising to the landlord for them not eating their ordered meal.

They both threaded their way across the street to the car park and it was not very long before he had tucked her up in a rug in front of the fire. She was so exhausted that she fell asleep almost immediately.

Joe telephoned the office and truthfully stated that Erin was ill and that he had brought her home and would stay with her until her mother arrived to look after both her and Miles as Max was away. He thought that would pacify the staff as he knew they were all extremely concerned about her, but in his heart he knew that they would all come to their own conclusions and eventually guess as they all knew about Max and his antics. There was no need for them all to know all the full facts, they would all have their own problems to deal with and some would also have their own skeletons in the cupboard too.

In the following few months, Joe continued to be very supportive to both Erin and Miles. They spent many happy hours together tripping off into the country, fishing, rambling, canoeing and these times reminded Joe wistfully of days gone by when he and Bob had done the same things with David. He tried not to become too attached to the boy. Nothing here he felt would be permanent and he did not wish to become too involved with either of them. Nevertheless, he did find himself spending less time at home. He anticipated that Trudie knew where he was going but she never commented at any time. There were never any confrontations as there would surely have been under normal circumstances, and for that he was grateful.

By now it was unwritten, and unsaid, that they would both proceed to do their own thing, only going out together on the very rarest of occasions.

His relationship with Erin had remained for a long time on a purely platonic basis, but it was inevitable that at sometime things could change.

Everyone knew that it was very unlikely that Max would be coming back. They realised that a loving relationship had blossomed between Joe and Erin, and this was now accepted. The staff had thought that it was a happy solution for both of them, and with only a few comical comments being made, in the kindest possible way, the staff felt that they both deserved some happiness.

One night the firm had tripped off on a social outing to a local brewery. Everyone had partaken, and had more than their fill of all the liquid freebies available to them in a short space of time.

The coach had dropped everyone off in the town centre and they had hailed a taxi to take them back to Erin's house. Miles was staying overnight with his paternal grandparents, who could not do enough to compensate for their errant son's misdemeanours and the child was staying with them for the whole weekend to give Erin some prime time to herself.

Erin coaxed Joe to stay overnight. He was tired and a tiny bit tipsy and needed little persuasion so he did not object. It was inevitable that one thing would lead to another and it did and a wondrous night of lovemaking ensued both feeling the need for physical closeness and fulfilment after being so long celibate.

The morning brought no embarrassment or reproaches. They both knew that initially the drink had brought down all their inhibitions and exhibited their physical needs. The feeling of loving and not being in love with one another was mutual, both knew that each had always had a heavy respect and real fondness in their relationship.

The liaison proved fine for both of them. It suited them perfectly, and lasted for almost two years in the same vein, each giving comfort and support to the other at a time when it was essentially needed.

It was at the end of the second summer that Erin confessed to Joe that for the last four weeks she had been receiving letters and telephone calls from Max in Alberta.

He had been apologising profoundly and profusely for all the hurt and agony that he had put her through and that lately he had been missing her and Miles terribly. He had made a terrible mistake but he had needed that time to take stock. It had been essential to him as he had been at breaking point, but that now he had sorted himself out. Could she possibly forgive him? Could she think seriously about joining him in Canada where he was now well established in his own business which was prospering by the day?

It had always been obvious to Joe that she loved the man deeply. He was her soul mate, the love of her life and she could overlook the discrepancies in his make up to just be with him.

She had put her house on the market and would be flying out to be with him in just ten days time and could Joe forgive her?

As far as Joe was concerned there was nothing to forgive. He had always felt that it would be inevitable that she would forgive Max and return to him if she were given the chance and that chance was now here and he was not proved wrong. They had both been there for each other at a time when they both needed solace. There had never been any serious 'do or die' commitment. There was absolutely nothing here to hold her and he envied the fact that even though the love of her life was not reliable, she had at least still got the enviable word 'LOVE' in her life, which was something that no one at all could ever take away from her.

So, on a sunny Friday morning he waved her, and her excited child off, as he stood on the observation platform at Heathrow Airport. She promising to keep in touch but he not knowing if would ever see her again, but elated in the fact that for now at least she was ecstatically happy.

Chapter Seven

Life after Erin went on pretty much the same and Joe sank into a kind of discontented contentment, accepting that the life that he had was the life that he would always have and there was really very little that he could do about it except go on as he was. Fate is always lying just around the corner, albeit, whether for good or for bad. It was waiting again for Joe with a vengeance.

It was a lousy wet and dismal Tuesday afternoon and Joe had been out to see a client about some discrepancy in his accounts. He had just taken off his coat when the telephone rang and he picked up the receiver.

A women, whose voice he could not recognise, was garbling a profusion of unidentifiable words into the telephone. He listened intently, trying to pick up the message for some seconds before he had to raise his voice and stop her in her tracks and ask her to calm down and repeat what she had said.

The woman would have been understandably shocked at the firmness in his voice, and had halted for some seconds, until she realised that she would have to calm down in order to make him understand what she had to say.

"It's me, Joe. Cissy. Cissy Blackstock", she almost screamed, "You have to come home immediately!"

"Calm down, Cissy", Joe said quietly realising that she was extremely upset to say the least.

An icy hand reached under his shirt and clutched his heart as he tried to control any panic that seemed to be rising within him. His parents' next door neighbour would not be contacting him without good reason.

"Why should I come home?" he enquired and groaning knowing full well that she meant 'home' to his parents' house and not his own.

"I can't explain over the telephone but you should come home, and now!" She placed the receiver down before he could ask any further questions.

Was it his father or his mother? Were they ill or worse? Without hesitation he picked up his coat and felt to ensure his wallet was there with enough money and credit cards to see him alright. He stepped into the outer office and dictated notes to his secretary about business and asked her to inform Trudie that he had to go up to Yorkshire at very short notice. He would contact her later when he knew more to tell her and with that he found himself in the car speeding quickly north and a great feeling of foreboding enshrouding his very being.

Apart from stopping for petrol halfway up the M1, Joe never remembered any of the journey to Yorkshire from Nottingham. A robot mind had driven him there whilst he had relived explanations as to why he was going there at all. His imagination running riot and wildly out of control.

His relief at getting there in one piece, and so quickly, was outweighed by what he was about to learn when he actually arrived. He was ignorant of the facts and had absolutely no idea what to expect. He drove straight from the motorway, and when he arrived at his parent's house he immediately parked his car in their drive as the gates had been left open in readiness for his arrival. He rapidly alighted to find his father silhouetted in the doorway of the lighted hallway with his arms outstretched, his face contorted with anguish and obviously waiting for the comfort and joy of his son's embrace. Without words he clutched Joe for a few seconds and then gently led him into the house.

Joe had been impatient to find out what was wrong but his father could not be rushed. He was too inconsolable and Joe had to be tolerant.

Cissy Blackstock was still there, and waiting with a sweet, strong cup of tea. She apologised for not being forthcoming over the telephone, but Bob had insisted that she tell Joe nothing at all until he arrived when he could hear it all face to face from his father. All Cissy could do was to look exceptionally grim and keep rolling her eyes and shaking her head.

In the end after taking some time to be able to talk Bob started to relate the horrifying details about what had befallen his beloved Celia. Even though Joe had anticipated that his mother had suffered some kind of accident the horror of it clouded his face as the gruesome details enfolded.

Celia had retired from nursing some time ago, but it had not stopped her from helping in the community. It was part and parcel of her make up. She could not sit still for very long and felt that her age mattered not as far as continuing with the things she liked to do most. She was very popular and much sought after. Indeed, a lot of the people would come and see Celia before they even thought about going to see their doctor, and she in turn was pleased that she could be of assistance to them.

Today had apparently been no exception. She had been asked by an ex colleague to meet her at the house of a cantankerous old lady, who would only do as she was asked if Celia asked her. The present nurses had great difficulty with her, and Celia knew all the right buttons to press to get her to do as they asked and she had agreed to meet her there.

Apparently, Bob had not wanted her to go due to the inclement weather but because she had insisted he had offered to drive her there. She had declined, stating that she did not want him to be sitting around in the car as he might catch a chill. She had set off from home mid morning and was making her way to the woman's house when an old patient of Celia's suffering from dementia had drifted out of his house, unknown by his daughter, who was his carer, and made off down the road. Celia had been driving up the road when Edgar had suddenly decided to cross over and not having the sense, or the wherewithal, to look out for traffic had just stepped off the pavement without hesitation and proceeded to cross the road. The road was icy. Celia swerved.

She missed him, but skidded on the black ice and ploughed straight into the railings of the local school. One of the rails projectiled through the windscreen and impaled her straight through her heart and onto the seat. She never had a chance.

The police doctor had assured Bob that her death would have been instantaneous but neither Bob or Joe could find any consolation in that fact, as they could imagine her horror in the split seconds before her death.

The hours that followed his father's revelation of all the terrible details were passed with both Joe and him gazing stupidly into the fire which expelled the only light in the otherwise unlit room. Joe's hand cupping his father's over the arm of the chair. Both men saying nothing. Their minds obviously recapitulating on the events of their lives and the repeated memory of the unbelievable and cataclysmic happenings of the day. The fact that his mother was no longer a person, but a cold cadaver, lying on a mortuary slab. Neither men rose to go to bed and both slept, fitfully, on and off in their chairs all night long.

They both awoke to the light of dawn with stiff and aching limbs. The intense pain of grief as the full extent of the previous day's horrors hit them both once again. They both took turns to bathe and feeling more refreshed came downstairs to the smell of bacon, eggs, toast and the aroma of coffee drifting towards them from the kitchen.

Cissy was sombrely going about her chores, knowing full well that if she did not at least try to tempt them with some morsel of food they would probably not even think about breakfast. She knew that they would need some sustenance to be able to tackle all the to-ing and fro-ing they would have no option but to undertake that day.

Both men made a real effort to smile in their appreciation of her thoughtfulness. She was, and always had been, a very kind neighbour and a friend to all of them. So much so that they had all in turn almost made her part of the family as she had lost her own husband in the war and never re-married. Without children of her own she had always made such a fuss of Joe. Today was no exception and Joe was very grateful. She was aghast at what had happened, but was glad that she could be of some comfort to them.

Without any appetite at all the men ate their meal. They would not have upset Cissy by rejecting it and thanked her for her thoughtfulness. It really was good to know she was there. Someone else to talk to other than themselves, as there was only so much that they could say without being repetitive and after a while that would be tedious.

The day went by calling at the Police station, the Doctor's, the Registrar's and the Funeral Director's and so on. All the necessary things that had to be done. Of course, there would have to be a Post Mortem and an Inquest, but everything looked cut and dried as there had been many witnesses to the accident. It was, more or less an established understanding that the verdict would be accidental death. It would be no consolation for losing her, but it was a fact that would have to be accepted by them both.

Trudie had taken the news in her usual way. There were no surprises there. She drove up to Yorkshire and called in to see Joe and Bob. A visit which lasted all of ten minutes, but it was enough for them. Neither men would have expected her, nor wanted her to be hypocritical. She had then departed to stay with her parents until the actual funeral had taken place. After contacting some of her old cronies who were mostly old clients, she would drift off again back to her life in Nottingham, without another thought for either of them. She would, in her opinion have been a dutiful wife and that was enough for her.

In the days that followed Joe took his father out fishing, bowling, walking out on the moors and country pubs. It was therapeutic for both of them and a real treat for them to spent some luxury time together.

The funeral had been harrowing. Celia was very popular and throngs of people turned up as a mark of respect, all being very supportive but no one knowing what to say, which was understandable, Joe could relate to that. He knew they all cared and he appreciated all their kindnesses knowing full well that they could do nothing more than they were already doing.

Celia's ex colleague and Edgar's daughter were totally grief stricken because of that old phenomenon of feeling guilty with the 'if only' complex, but Bob and Joe assured them that they could not possibly think that way. What will be…and all that.

Keith and Sally had come up to Yorkshire from Devon for the funeral. This was so appreciated by Joe and he was so overwhelmed to see his beloved old friend that he could not contain his joy at seeing him and indeed Sally, who he always liked and admired. The infusion of both joy and grief resulted in Joe actually breaking down and shedding his first tears since David's death. It was as though he no longer had any control over his emotions and he felt embarrassed at his failure to contain himself, but forgave himself for the weakness as he realised that Keith's wise words were right. "There is only so much a human being can take without reaching breaking point. Everyone is supposed to be provided with a safety valve, otherwise we would all end up as mad as hatters!"

Joe had stayed with his father for a full two weeks after the funeral and the inquest were over, then he had returned to Nottingham. He returned to Yorkshire for weekends once every fortnight to be with Bob and telephoned him regularly. They became closer than ever and needed each other for various reasons of support. Joe began to realise that Yorkshire was where his roots were and felt uneasy and restless when he knew he would have to return to Nottingham after every weekend in Yorkshire.

As if by some miracle, someone 'up there' could read his thoughts, because not many months had passed before he had to attend an accountants convention at the Barbican Centre in London.

He had met many nice colleagues over the years and one in particular, Cecil Brinkley, came over to him with a very friendly attitude and some exciting suggestions.

Cecil had an opening for a senior accountant, with a view to a directorship in his firm of Brinkley and Mather, in Wakefield, and would Joe be interested? They would make it worth his while financially and deal with any expenses incurred during removals and house buying.

Usually, Joe had to be convinced and cajoled and talked into such propositions before making any too drastic moves, but now he had no objections or hesitations at all. He explained his eagerness to accept to a bemused and bewildered Cecil, who was astonished at the rapidity of Joe's acceptance. He had never before settled anything with such alacrity in his life and was very happy with Joe's decision as time was of the essence for everyone in Wakefield and a sharp response was what he had hoped for but dared not contemplate, he was quite prepared for Joe to think about it and let him know at a later date.

It appeared that everyone was happy, but would Trudie be? It mattered not!

....

The house in Nottingham sold surprisingly quickly and even though he was eager to return to Yorkshire, Joe was very sad to have to say his goodbyes to all the very good friends he had made in Nottingham, especially his colleagues who had remained solid supports during his years of traumas. He hoped sincerely that he would see them all again at some time in the future.

With a brand new set of golf clubs slung over his shoulder, given as a generous leaving gift, he fondly waved his goodbyes as he opened his car door and blew a teasing kiss to the women who were watching him leave from their upstairs windows.

Trudie had said little regarding their move to Yorkshire. She had not entirely objected, but had not seemed overjoyed either, which did not entirely surprise Joe. He had no urge to discuss it with her. For once in his married life he was doing exactly what he wanted to do, without any thought for her or how she actually felt.

They moved quickly into the newly built house. It was not overly large. Just a moderate sized semi detached in a small private cul de sac on the verge of the town but it had a pleasant rural outlook and the gardens had been landscaped for them so that was easy to manage from the onset.

Trudie apparently had managed to contact most of her old clients and some of them had never lost touch with her. They appeared to be happy enough for her to continue her business with them. Joe considered that she must have much more rapport and graciousness with them than she had ever had with him, or albeit, any of his friends. He did not care about that any more. They both had their own lives.

Joe settled in at Brinkley and Mathers immediately. The staff were friendly and more to the point very competent and more than capable to be left to their own devices without very much supervision.

The clients were a joy and complaints from them were few but then again the company did have a wonderful reputation. This eased many business owners' worries by their information and efficiency. Joe wished he could have been here years ago.

It was not until Joe had been in Yorkshire for a few months that he realised that his father was seeing less of him. Bob seemed as though he had accepted Celia's death and come to terms with it and was grateful to Cissy for sitting in with him on an evening, going shopping with him and for him, and tripping off on daily excursions. Indeed, they were good companions. Company for each other, and it relieved Joe's feelings of responsibility towards his father to a certain extent. If Bob was happy enough with the situation, then so was Joe.

The following February, true to form, Joe sent his letters off to his three old friends. Barry and family still in Australia, Frank and Ron still in Kenya, but now retired from the Police Force and both undertaking security jobs for banks in Nairobi.

Joe had more to tell them this year. The tragedy of his mother's death. The more joyful news about his return to Yorkshire.

He knew they would think it hilarious as they had always teased him about his lack of adventure, but he knew they would be pleased for him anyway doing what he wanted, which was the main thing.

Their three letters dropped through the letter box one after the other over the next week, and were all handed to Joe by Trudie with a 'tut'. She making sure that Joe knew how she felt about his youthful pact so many years ago. Obviously, she felt that it was silly or ludicrous, but the mealy mouthed woman no longer frustrated him as she had with her suspicious destructive nature all borne in ignorance of her never really knowing her own husband.

The letters were all full of news and joy. Everyone seemed to be healthy and all appeared to be happy and all enjoying something that Joe would never have, grandchildren. He envied them. He would have loved to have had the pleasure of grandchildren as his own father had had with David. His eyes misted over. He should go out and stay with them, goodness knows he had been invited enough times. His pulse raced at the exciting thought of such trips and without any other thought or hesitation he turned to speak to Trudie.

"What do you think about a trip to Australia? Then next year perhaps a trip to Kenya?" The words tumbled out of his mouth like an excited schoolboy.

No response.

"Did you hear me Trudie?" he asked.

"Of course I heard you", she snapped back.

The ice in her voice had made the back of his neck prickle. "If I go on holiday Joe, it will not be with you. It would most certainly not be to see your old chums from your Army days!" She continued "Them taking you around to see all their families. Children running around everywhere, barbecues on an evening and down to the beach. Hmm.. Not for me", she sneered and turned to face him now. Her face showing an expression of gloating and the creases exhibiting a metamorphosis of all the years of nasty expressions oozing out from within.

Joe sat silently for a moment and then felt the need to say something he had wanted to say for a long time to ease the years of self control that he had endured at her hands.

"You know I have never asked for very much from you Trudie. I gathered from the start that our marriage was not going to be the best in world. We are both of us, what we are, even if we are not we ought to be! I have never given you much grief. I never visualised, however, that you would want to be married and live the life of a single woman or a widow. Tell me truthfully. Did you marry me wholly for social standing because you were pregnant or did you really want to marry me?"

At one time he would have been apprehensive as to what kind of reaction he would have got, but he was past that predicament by now and waited hopefully for a truthful answer. At the same time acknowledging that he had never had one before and was probably expecting too much.

Her answer came forth directly and without hesitation. It was as though now the time was right for confrontations and truths would be told no matter what the consequences would be. Without any hint of humility in her voice she erupted into a barrage of damning confession.

"No. I really did not wish to marry you, and yes, I did marry you because I was pregnant". She smirked slightly before she continued and Joe remained silent.

"I will tell you a story, shall I? Seeing as you really want to know, but, don't blame me when it is told because I always thought that it would be better for you if you were never told it. I didn't think that you could handle it".

Joe prickled in anticipation of what he could possibly learn during this rare journey into truthfulness with this gauche and nefarious woman.

She continued, "The story is about a girl who never had much time for boys at all. She thought that they were stupid and infantile even when they grew into men. Nevertheless, she dated them, because that was the thing to do and eventually she started going out seriously with a boy who had good connections and an ambition to have a successful future. That was enough for most girls, and was certainly enough for this girl, so she persevered and tolerated the relationship with the hope that her determination would bear fruit and that they would marry when his studies were completed and he had graduated. Well, everything went according to plan for quite some time, then the young man decided that he wanted to end their relationship and that, would be the best for both of them. Well, the girl was not going to have any of that, and knowing that the young man could be easily persuaded to succumb to her sexual advances, she seduced him, with the full intention of becoming pregnant and trapping him into marriage whether he would want to or not. Everything went according to plan. The girl managed to conceive. The only thing was though, that when she told her ex lover, he did not believe her. He thought she was lying to trap him, and told her in no uncertain words never to contact him again. You can guess that the girl was in somewhat of a predicament, especially in the 'fifties'. It would not matter one iota if it were now, but then…She had to improvise and find another alternative and quickly…I think that by now you will know the rest and so I will not reiterate further".

She stood there facing him, expressionless, flat and emotionless waiting for his response. Her secret was now out, now said, the outcome had been verbally horrendous.

Joe's initial reaction was virtually the same as it had been all those years ago when she had told him she was pregnant. He felt that there was no way that he could side step this predicament and keep his sanity. He felt like a contemptible wimp who had his limitations and had to fight with all his strength not to rise from the chair and strike her dead.

Every action she had ever undertaken had been tactical and planned with cold precision. She had purposely seduced him that fateful night of Trevor Watson's party to complete her purpose. She had only wished for the comfort and security of her marital status and title, so much so that she had never allowed him to have the benefit of the truth which would have enabled him to make a choice of having another life, giving him happiness, children and some essence of normality.

His life had been forfeit, and used cruelly for another's purpose. He was repulsed by her audacity and more disgusted at himself for being so easily beguiled, so trusting, so naive. It was an extremely bitter taste to imbibe.

She had committed a violation of marital rights and expectancies and determined from the onset to cause misery by her selfish attitude to men, her own son among them. He had been caught up in a chain of events, a vortex of circumstances, a contradiction of all he had ever held dear. He had been there. He was the fall guy. He felt the need for revenge, retribution and vengeance but he was relying on his self control to win again in the end, she was not worth it.

"My son, David, was not my son?" Joe choked on the words, was there no end to his misery?

"His father was Trevor Watson, although Watson never knew", she hissed triumphantly. "He never had the satisfaction of knowing him. Serves him right", she smirked.

Biological parentage had never been the issue, because, Joe in his naivety, had never questioned it. There had been no chance of D.N.A. proof at that time, and blood tests were unreliable. A proof of pregnancy note from the doctor had to suffice in those days.

The confession had done nothing to quell the love he had always felt for David, nor did it, or would it, make him grieve any less. The fact that she had so cruelly used them all as a means to an end and not even permitted Joe to have a child of his own was more than he could bear.

His face contorted into an indescribable torrent of emotional torment and obvious agony on learning the truth and the facts of things. He did not deserve a fraction of this kind of treatment and without another word he left the house.

………………………........

Robert Bullimore sat and listened intently, silent and gravely serious as Joe retold the story. As the full facts enfolded he started to cry. Joe placed his hand on his in order to console him knowing how disappointed he would also be to learn that David was not his biological grandson.

"She is a cruel and evil woman, that Trudie, Joe", he started, "but if this is a day for confessions, then I have one also. It will ease my pain greatly if I tell you, but you have to forgive us, your mother and I, because we thought that it would be for the best".

Joe's eyes widened. "You knew?"

"We had a good idea. Your mother was a midwife and knew a full term baby when she saw one, and David was full term, meaning that you could not have possibly been his father, Joe. Your mother and I knew the anguish you had gone through before you married Trudie. We saw that you were delighted with the baby and we both felt that we should not enlighten you for everyone's sake. How wrong could we have been?" His father's tormented body writhed in anguish at the thought of his Joe being deceived by so many people and even those who loved him the most.

Joe could identify with why his parents had hidden the true facts from him. They had had the best intentions but they had inadvertently done him no favours. Nothing would have changed between David and himself. Indeed, he would probably have loved the boy more if that had been possible, for him being used in that way.

All these years Joe had secretly cursed Trevor Watson for not marrying Trudie, which would have allowed Joe to have found the love and happiness he so nostalgically yearned for and always felt that he could possibly have had with Leah. Now, in a strange way, he pitied him, for never having known of his son's existence. Of David's wonderful personality and charisma. Joe, at least had had that proud privilege and he would always be grateful for that and could always cherish that thought. But if he had known… his life would have changed. He could have had a life. This was just an existence. Now things were going to have to definitely change. Every dog has it's day if it can wait long enough and Joe had waited long enough!

…………………….......

Reuben and Lottie McDonald had always returned to Barbados every other year for holidays, but mostly to see their families. They had both emigrated from there to Britain as children after the end of the war.

Reuben had been a great friend and colleague of Joe's for all his time in Nottingham, they still kept in touch on a regular basis. Even so, it was a real surprise to Joe when Reuben telephoned one evening and asked him if he would like a holiday in Barbados with just him? Apparently, Lottie was originally going to go but had decided not to because their daughter was due to have a baby. She felt that she would be more settled if she was around to support her. Lottie was insisting that Reuben should still go, and suggested that he ask Joe as it would be good for him and the trip was all paid for, not that Joe would not compensate them anyway.

Well, it was not Australia or Kenya but the offer was so well meant, and he liked Reuben immensely. He would not have offended him for the world and so he gladly accepted even though it was very short notice.

Joe realised that it would be a great relief to leave reality behind him. By the end of that week both men were soaring across the Atlantic ocean and anticipating a wonderful warm and sunny holiday in the Caribbean. They were not to be disappointed.

The next two weeks were idyllic. Blue skies and bluer sea, white sands, swaying palms and the rest that one expects from a paradise island. Joe was welcomed by everyone like a long lost son and it was obvious from the way they spoke that Reuben had spoken of him often, which made him feel confidently comfortable. He was very flattered.

Everywhere they went that holiday and everyone they visited feasted them with the most delicious food Joe had ever tasted. The island's music was played everywhere with smiling faces. Joe never once saw anyone looking glum or morose and wondered what their secret was. Everything was so refreshing and new to him, so tranquil and calm. No rush or calamity. Such a tonic. He would never be able to repay them enough, such lovely thoughtful people.

Reuben's reward was enough just to see Joe laughing and joking all the while with his family and friends, who it was clear to see, Reuben adored.

Everyone knew that Joe was not a happy man, but he was a nice man, and everyone liked him. He was very popular and on this holiday had turned out to be a perfect companion.

A cousin of Reuben's had taken them both out scuba diving. Of course, Reuben was an experienced diver, but Joe had to be taught, and it was an incredulous experience never to be forgotten. By the end of the holiday Joe had become quite an accomplished diver himself. The sheer magic of the adventure. The colours and the creatures were such a magnificent sight, one that had to be experienced at first hand to be appreciated. Millions of plants and species. No film or description could possibly do justice to the wonders he saw during that dreamy two weeks diving in the clear waters. To play with the fish, who volunteered to swim up to him and let him caress them, and small octopuses and squid gently entwining their tentacles around his limbs in exploration of the human creature, who in turn, were equally as alien to them as they were so strangely interesting to humans.

Joe was 'hooked' This was a pastime that he could easily indulge in regularly, and he was determined to practise again on future holidays.

All too soon the enchanting, magical holiday ended, leaving Joe feeling tanned and fit and refreshed beyond his wildest dreams. Even Reuben's black skin was darker than usual and the two men laughed when comparing as they were waved off from the airport by Reuben's many relatives like a couple of V.I.Ps.

The journey home seemed short, and it was a good flight, but the two friends had to part at Manchester airport to go their separate ways, both promising that they would try and repeat the experience another time. Joe surely hoped so, it had been such a wonderful treat, which Reuben had wanted to give freely, but Joe insisted that he should be reimbursed and his friend fully understood that Joe would not accept anything for nothing. He had felt so happy to be the instigator of Joe's holiday, which had turned out to be so good for him and one for which Joe would be forever grateful and would never ever forget.

Chapter Eight

The offer of a job at Maddie's garage had proved heaven sent for Joe. It kept him occupied, in touch with the public and apart from maintaining his ongoing friendship with Maddie herself, it had given him the opportunity to start a very amicable alliance with Jack Hillman, the station manager.

Jack, who was about the same age, had much in common with Joe, even to the point of them taking advantage of their off time together, either fishing or golfing. All this time Joe managing very well to see a lot less of Trudie, which suited him down to the ground.

His life in general had peppered up. The dark despair that he had been drowning in of late was rapidly diminishing, and with the humour and humility of all those around him being infectious it would hopefully disappear altogether. This left him prevaricating as to why he had not negotiated such a solution to his problems earlier and eliminated much of his own miseries which he now felt could have been on the whole self inflicted. He had allowed Trudie to manipulate him, deviously, he would be the first to admit and so he pardoned himself putting it down to him being so trusting and vulnerable.

As a new optimism beckoned him, he became enveloped in the promise of a brighter future. He became stronger both mentally and physically. Born again. It was now up to him to ensure that he never took another backward step into the doom and gloom of the past. He felt a philosophical need to nourish the profound feeling that he still needed much variation in his life and would not deviate from that endeavour.

The shop door of the garage opened suddenly one sunny Monday morning. Jack Hillam marched in with a look of great sadness and disappointment clouding his usually smiling face.

He picked up his daily tabloid newspaper and walked over to the till. Neither men speaking at first, only their eyes meeting. Joe's eyebrow was turned up, silently asking the question "What was wrong?" and Jack eventually deciding to put him out of his misery started to explain.

The holiday they had booked for the next September, with another couple of friends, would either have to be cancelled or altered because his friend had suffered a heart attack the night before. There was no way that they would be able to continue with their plans as he would not be fit enough to go, if indeed he survived, as he would have to undergo surgery.

Jack's wife Catherine, was quite a timid woman, who needed the assurance of someone other than Jack being with them for security on the holiday should anything untoward happen whilst they were so far away from home.

Jack was devastated as he had looked forward to the holiday for a very long time and Catherine had taken some persuading to go in the first place.

Now she was panicking and the outcome of it all appeared to be a foregone conclusion.

A tour of the Eastern Seaboard of the United States of America had long been a dream of Joe's and the idea had been suggested to his father, Bob. Bob had felt that he was now too old to try out such a physically demanding journey and so the idea had been scrapped. Now perhaps the opportunity was there. He could fill in for the discrepancy of Jack's friends not being able to go.

The suggestion was made to Jack, whose eyes lit up like beacons at the thought of a solution to his predicament. He sighed and his shoulders drooped. "But your wife would not go, would she Joe?" he groaned in exasperation. "There is only a double room available and they will not consider it for a single person"

Joe grimaced and tried to think of other alternatives and then a voice softly whispered "Take me Joe. Take me!"

Joe's eyes widened. Maddie stood there in all her glory, a wide grin from ear to ear and her eyes shining with teasing enthusiasm.

Joe grinned back not knowing that she had been there and jokingly said, "Hey, that would be great but what would the neighbours say?"

"To hell with the neighbours. They would probably wish they were going instead of us. I'm not joking Joe, I MEAN IT, don't you know!!" Then she started to giggle which was so infectious they were all soon falling about with laughter, Joe's face flushing as the heat rose from his neck until it reached the roots of his hair. He could not remember the last time he had blushed, and felt somewhat embarrassed, but not for long, not with Maddie.

"I don't know what you overheard Maddie, but there is only one double room". Jack shrugged his shoulders for the umpteenth time at the apparent hopelessness of it all.

"I know, I heard Jack". She eyed both men watching for their response, and confidently continued. "We are both adults Joe. We live in a modern age. What does it matter?" Still waiting for a response that was not forthcoming from either of the men she continued on excitedly. "There will be twin beds I expect. We could make an arrangement for the bathroom. I'm not prudish. We could all have a whale of a time. We would never be short on conversation and we could have heaps of fun".

There was still a numb silence from both the men who were genuinely milling the proposition around in their minds and then she said "Well I'm waiting. Are you going to take me up on my offer or not? No pressure though".

The smile never left her lips and both she and Jack waited in anticipation of Joe's answer, Jack's face a picture of complete bewilderment.

"When can we go down to the agency to alter the booking?" Joe shouted out in excitement at last, surprising himself at his new found assertiveness. It had taken him several seconds to fully grasp that Maddie's offer was in fact genuine, and not some kind of jocular comment, but once the realisation dawned on him he had no hesitation in grasping the moment and the once in a lifetime opportunity.

They all three screamed out in excitement and almost started dancing around the shop. They arranged to all meet that afternoon and complete the bookings, Joe hardly able to contain himself. He could hardly wait.

Joe knew that Maddie's offer to go on the holiday was not just a sentimental gesture. He felt that her unspoken intention was to share his life up to a point and without asking anything from him that he could not in all conscience give at this particular time.

She had known when they had met that first time in the park that he was at breaking point She was determined to help him in every way that she could without prying too far into the reason why he had reached that point in the first place, whilst not appearing to be condescending which was the last thing she would want him to think. All that she was trying to do was to accelerate his complete recovery and bring him back to being the young man she had known all those years ago.

At the same time Joe felt that he could justify his actions to others, without reproach. He felt that there was no way that he would be making a fool of himself. No one would need to know anyway, but if they did, what did it matter. Maddie would only smile and be honest about the whole thing if asked, he knew that, and at one time that might have bothered him somewhat, but now he was beginning to feel and think like Maddie. It was a feeling of freedom and losing his inhibitions that he relished.

……………………….......

Once the paperwork had been adjusted and the booking confirmed, Joe lost no time in telling his father about the plans he had made for the following September, which was only a matter of ten weeks away. Bob was delighted at the prospect of his son's holiday. He liked Maddie. He had always liked her family in the old days and he silently wished that she and Joe could one day make a go of their relationship and put it on a more serious footing but he never commented. Best leave well alone in that direction, each to his own.

Joe knew that his father would back anything he intended to do, but was flabbergasted when Bob announced that he himself had decided to go away on a one week tour, to Eastbourne, with Cissy. They were also going to share a twin bedded room, (but, just for cheapness and companionship, you know to save on the single supplement!) hmmm..

The two men laughed impishly and in unison, both pleased at the same time for each other at their new found more intimate friendships. It was the most welcome contentment not experienced for a very long time, but both of them realising that life could be very fickle and cruel but that they must not be pessimistic and must grasp at any happiness offered to them whilst they could.

Joe never mentioned the holiday to Trudie. He felt that she had no right to know anything about his life at all. He had always been a patient and forgiving man but she had always interpreted this as a sign of weakness, and had made no secret of the fact that she felt he was repulsive to her in every way. This had previously made him feel very humiliated, dejected and depressed but now a new life for him was beckoning and he was embracing it with a new and wonderful confidence which was so refreshing, he was relishing it.

He decided that he would make no decisions before the holiday about his future, but had every intention of making one after he returned. He felt that his home was now a house he used only as living quarters and nothing else and he had no intention of continuing to endure things any longer as they had been.

…………………….......

Bob and Cissy's holiday had been a complete success. They both arrived back home, tanned and happy and full of tales of their escapades and the people they had met. Joe could not have been happier for them. His father had found another soul mate, and at the same time, had taken a load of responsibility away from Joe's own shoulders, by not needing as much support from him as he had done in the past.

The change in their circumstances had opened up a new dawn for Cissy also, who up to then had had quite a lonely life for many years but nevertheless, both his father and Cissy had made it explicitly clear that their relationship was of a platonic but loving nature and that all they really needed was the companionship of each other to combat the extreme loneliness they had both felt and endured previously. Joe could relate to that in every way, but it really was a great surprise for him to learn that they had both decided to live in one house and that house was to be Cissy's.

When Bob saw the look on Joe's face was one of amazement, he was pacified, because it was not one of displeasure. He gently took him aside and spoke to him as though he was still a young boy. "You have to understand Joe that this arrangement makes sense, economically as well as socially. We were both taking turns to visit and sit with each other every night and then getting up to go back to our own places and it all began to seem so futile. You know, Joe, just someone breathing in the same house if you wake up during the night, or when you rise in the mornings to greet you, makes the world of difference and the full realisation of this hit both of us during this holiday. We realised we would be coming back to the same routine as before, and so we decided to do something about it. Goodness knows, none of us know how long we have got or how long such a thing can last, and so we must snatch the moment whilst we can." Bob was looking pleadingly at his son, hoping that he would understand and give his blessing but he need not have fretted.

"You don't have to explain yourself to me Dad, you know that really. I understand only too well the feeling of complete loneliness and feel like you do, that you should grasp any happiness that comes your way, and of course you have my complete approval, not that you need it. You know that I like Cissy. I always have and I am as happy for her as I am for you. She deserves some happiness herself".

Joe smiled radiantly and hugged his father ferociously. He loved him so very much and was so delighted that he had found contentment so late in his life.

"I will not be selling the house for quite some while, Joe", Bob continued.

"You mean, just in case..?" Joe started.

"No. Not what you are thinking. I have no doubts on that score. I just thought that maybe, just maybe mind you, that you might wish to consider living here yourself when you return from America. You never know...anyway, the option is open to you to do just what you want. We'll see"

Joe's heart leapt. Bless him. Bob was still thinking for him, trying to solve his problems, providing other options but it was an option that Joe was more than willing to consider.

Maddie was thrilled when Joe told her of his father's intentions and thought that Bob's proposition about his house for Joe's use was a brilliant idea, but no plans were made in that direction at that time as the holiday was nearing fast and there were plenty of other things to organise without needing any further distractions. Joe did not, as usual want to do anything on the spur of the moment. He needed to take his time. Immediately after the holiday would be fine.

……………………........

Joe had packed his suitcase and hand luggage and left them at the foot of the stairs, in the hallway the previous night all ready for his early start in the morning. He had advised Trudie courteously that he would be away for the next sixteen days, not that he thought that he should really extend her that courtesy, but only to ensure that she did not misinterpret his movements and think hopefully that he was leaving her in the long term. He wished to ascertain that he would be given that privilege at a later date, but for the moment that brief information rendered should suffice and like as always she never commented one way or the other, just as she never had when he had gone to Barbados. She did not care in any way.

The taxi was prompt the following morning, having picked up Jack and Catherine first, which was just as well as he had not wanted Trudie to even catch a glimpse of Maddie at this point in time. Any gossip about them both was irrelevant but could wait until they returned. By then he would be strong enough to handle anything, he was sure of that.

Joe had never felt so excited about anything in his whole life. It was as if he had been reborn. He had always loathed flying, but at this moment he hadn't a care in the world, and was on a real high.

Once Maddie had been picked up in the taxi everyone laid back in the cab, which was large and comfortable and ran smoothly and silently along the busy M.62. Everyone was relaxed, even Catherine, who showed no signs at all of nerves at the thought of the one hour flight from Manchester to Heathrow, then the seven hour flight from there to New York. When the car eventually drew up at the internal flights departure terminal at Manchester airport, all four of them were bright and ready for their New England and Canadian adventure.

Chapter Nine

Catherine commented that it would have been nice to have travelled first class or even club class, as they all passed through the more luxurious accommodation on their way to the main tourist compartment of the Jumbo Jet, which was much more cramped and less comfortable than they had anticipated or would have preferred, but beggars cannot be choosers. People only get what they pay for and they all felt very privileged as it was to be embarking on this type of holiday at all. With a contented shrug they all tried to shrink into their numbered seats and belted up in preparation for the journey.

The cabin crew started to pamper them immediately with blankets and little packs containing socks, toothbrushes and paste and all the little necessities they might need on their journey, with the compliments of the airline. Without any delays they were off, soaring upwards into the clouds and soon levelling off for their flight across the great Atlantic ocean to the exciting continent beyond.

The flight was good with not a hint of turbulence. The film was excellent and the food was tasty. Each of them either reading, watching, completing puzzles or napping and the journey seemed to be over in no time at all as they touched down at J.F. Kennedy airport in good time and to a lovely, September Indian summer climate.

Once through the baggage section and passport control, a smart woman was waving a book in front of all the passengers and before very long people were emerging from all sides of the airport arrival lounge in unison and all identifying with the Tour Manager's colourful book of the advertised tour.

Everyone trailed their luggage behind them as they all followed her obediently to the exit of the airport, not wishing to be mislaid, where they were all led to a magnificent looking tour coach and a grinning driver welcoming them and arranging to take care and responsibility of everyone's precious cargoes.

The Tour Manager introduced herself as Jessica Nicholls and the driver was just 'Bill'.

'Just Bill' never said anything very much at all for the duration of the holiday, but always remained very jolly, friendly and extremely helpful and never but never complained. He worked extremely hard, driving from one city to another, loading luggage and unloading luggage and touring around, excursions of National interest and never appearing to have very much sleep at all.

Jessica, on the other hand, was absolutely full of personality and conversation and could negotiate every move with extreme and faultless timing between one place and the next without anyone suffering one seconds boredom on the long distances between one city and another. Her knowledge even though it was her job was absolutely astonishing and even though she must have repeated the same things over and over again to different tourists and travelled over the same ground many times, the repetitive nature of the work never showed up in her attitude, it was always as though this was her first tour and her enthusiasm for the tour never faltered or diminished.

From the very start of the holiday when they left the airport, everything was exciting for Joe. They travelled via Queens and Brooklyn and on into the Battery and

155

Manhattan island and their coach had come to a smooth stop outside a beautiful hotel practically next door to the World Trade Centre, and across the road from Wall Street and the Dow Jones building. The party had all alighted from the coach and were ushered into the hotel and the keys were quickly administered from the reception desk. Before they realised it Joe and Maddie were well ensconced in their room, gasping at the enormous size and luxury of it.

They were both greatly impressed and felt that this must be some wonderful omen to start off their great adventure.

The luggage had been delivered promptly to all the rooms of the tourists. Free porterage was included in the price of the trip, which was a welcome relief, as all their baggage was cumbersome and heavy. Everyone without exception, quickly bathed and changed and all went their separate ways to try and find inviting restaurants as practically all the Hotels in the United States did not provide meals for their guests. It did not matter as it felt good to stretch ones legs and explore the locality as it was still only eight o'clock in the evening, but they did not forget that it would be one o'clock in the morning at home, and they were all very tired after such a long day. After a substantial meal they all felt that it would be good to get to bed in decent time as they would all have much to see the following day.

Joe had smiled as he left the bathroom that night, he had been talking non stop about the days events until he had realised that he had been talking to himself as Maddie was sound asleep. He climbed into bed. Never mind, there would be plenty of time for talking in the next two weeks. Joe could not remember a time when he had felt so relaxed as he drifted into a deep and contented sleep.

…………………….........

Every day would be mapped out for them but that was why they had all booked this type of holiday, to be able to see as much as they possibly could in the time allocated.

They all knew that it would be tiring but they were all perfectly willing to put up with any inconveniences incurred without any complaints.

They all awoke early the next day to sunshine and a very comfortable warmth which meant that they would not be encumbered with coats and jackets. They walked across the road and around the corner to sit for a short while in a small park alongside the Hudson River with an easy view of the famous Statue of Liberty, which was situated at the mouth of that great river, and stood on a small island about ten acres in area. What most people had forgotten was the fact that it had once been used as a lighthouse.

A small café quite nearby had provided them with a light breakfast before they all met up with the coach for a short sharp excursion around New York City, before being dropped off at the harbour to see some performing dancers from Louisiana in their national dress and ending up with lunch on the quayside.

The afternoon was spent back in Manhattan and Joe and Jack obediently left the ladies who wanted to shop around in Macy's and Bloomingdale's. They in turn decided to have a gander at Madison Square Gardens and meander through some of the streets before they met up again with the ladies at the Mall.

Maddie and Catherine greeted the two men with smiles as they appeared with carrier bags full of goodies and boasted that they had managed to pick up one or two free items on the trip, courtesy of the tourist board.

Joe was delighted with everything and every moment, he had never had the joy and privilege of being with such a happy, excited normal woman before and the experience was intoxicating. He clung on to every second with a new enthusiasm, it was like being charged with electric.

After bathing and changing, that night the coach picked them all up again from the hotel and took them first to Greenwich Village where they sought out a restaurant for dinner which had all the atmosphere one would associate with such a lively cosmopolitan area. It was not until they were all tucking into their meal that they realised that this was a bar-restaurant full of females and that the females were all, in fact, males. They had all wandered inadvertently into this beautiful establishment without realising that they were among the gay and transvestite community, but were all made extremely welcome and enjoyed the meal immensely, with the proprietors doing more laughing than themselves at their initial but evident mistake.

Once back on the coach they were all treated to an extensive tour around the city by night. Forty second Street, Broadway, the very upper class Lexington Avenue and equally expensive Fifth Avenue, past Bergdorfs, Sachs, Tiffany's, down 59th Street to Central Park, on to Trump's Tavern, Time Square, the United Nations Building and the lovely Rockefeller Centre, which, when iced over in the wintertime catered for skaters and in summertime was the rendezvous for many a person wishing to just meander through the lovely gardens.

After visiting the observation tower on top of the Empire State building and seeing the Chrysler building from that height at night and the rest of New York illuminated, everyone could only gasp at the spectacle. Up to now, they had only seen such things on American films. The feeling was awesome and scary to say the least.

Joe's legs felt weak and he dare not comment for fear of being thought of as a softie, but he need not have bothered as almost everyone commented once on the ground again about the same kind of feelings.

The night's outing ended with a spectacular view of an illuminated Manhattan from the Brooklyn Bridge, which was not very far from their hotel and if the holiday had to end now, no one would have been disappointed, as it had all been so fulfilling.

Almost like the night before, Joe and Maddie had practically fallen straight asleep after long soaks in the bath following a very hectic and wonderful day in the city where presumably no one ever sleeps.

They arose the next morning early, as instructed, boarded the coach for the two hundred and twenty mile journey from New York to Boston, Massachusetts, following a route which took them through Hoboken in New Jersey, which immediately started Joe reminiscing about his great idol Frank Sinatra, being born there. Then on to Long Island, Connecticut, on past Yale University and all the places of great interest like the homes of the Kennedys and the Fitzgeralds until they finally arrived in Boston in time for a late lunch which was taken whilst exploring the lovely Quincy market.

The sun was reigning down upon them as they ate and laughed and discussed seeing the three hundred years old clock in the church, reputed to be the oldest working clock in the United States, and the two hundred year old sailing ship, lovingly named 'Old Ironside' by the Bostonians, besides all the other marvellous things they had seen so far and everyone with great enthusiasm for what lay ahead.

Joe and Maddie were tactfully left by Catherine and Jack to have a little privacy that evening, as the afternoon had been full of the usual tourism places of interest, and 'following the guide', could be a little breathtaking at times, trying to fit in all the sights.

They decided to stroll along to the Mall which stayed open until quite late and was famed for many different kinds of restaurants. Their choice that evening was Italian, and very enjoyable, followed by a gentle meander afterwards through the streets and back to their hotel, which was quiet and relaxing and gave them time to talk, mostly about what they had seen, and were looking forward to seeing, but eventually drifting off in a more personal vein and as like almost always with a hint of nostalgia about their early past as they could always find much to talk about, sometimes sad but sometimes very funny.

Tragedies of some kind can hit almost every household. How people cope with such traumas and keep their sanity no one knows. Like little Will, Maddie's seven year old brother, who died after battling bravely with Infantile Paralysis in an Iron Lung which was quite commonplace in those days. Her sisters, Beth and Sadie had survived chronic bouts of measles but were left with hearing defects.

All very sad times but everyone coming through with happy faces and carrying on as best they could under extremely hard circumstances.

…………………………........

Unfortunately, they all woke up to rain the following day, but no one was fazed and everyone continued to smile as they all departed early morning for their journey up to Quebec in Canada, through the White Mountains, in New Hampshire and on to the Green Mountains of Vermont. On again, through the Appalachian Range, which stretched fifteen hundred miles from the Blue Ridge Mountains of Virginia and up to Quebec where in 1623 the English established their first colony. Where half the original hundred Pilgrims died and the friendly Red Indians who lived in that area helped, fed and sheltered the other half in order for them to survive the very harsh winter. Thus was the start of the annual American 'Thanksgiving' celebrations on the 23rd of November, and 9th October in Canada, both stemming from this area all those years ago. The tourists' minds went haywire trying to imagine the hardships they had all suffered.

As they travelled, there was glorious splendour everywhere. The clear and unpolluted lakes. The rivers and the white water rapids. The mountains. Beautiful red foliage, displayed mainly by the maple trees in their autumn dress. The tourists enjoyed viewing the picturesque buildings, with names mostly inherited from England.

They motored into Quebec across the mighty St, Lawrence River, which they were told spanned sixty miles across at its broadest point. They were soon signing the register at their latest hotel.

After a hot shower and a change of clothing they were all taken by 'Just Bill', their driver, in the coach to dine at the La Concorde, a rotating tower restaurant, overlooking the magnificent Chateau Frontenac, which was illuminated and stood grandly prominent over the historic city.

Again the meal was absolutely wonderful, enjoyed by all whilst listening to the tinkling piano keys of the resident pianist, playing soft ballads as everyone relaxed in the subdued atmosphere.

Quebec everyone was told was pronounced 'Kiebeck' by the French Canadians and was 386 miles from Boston, and so it was no real wonder that they were all so tired again after their meal and so with a welcome nightcap off they were again, asleep at the drop a hat.

The day afterwards was spent exploring the beautiful and quaint city in the autumn sunshine and mentally re-living the sometimes savage historic past.

Sometimes, Maddie could see that Joe's imagination was running riot, and in all the while that the little party had been holidaying, Joe had never noticed that Maddie had been assessing his every move and mood. She had been very clever at hiding the fact from him as she knew that he would have been very self conscious and constantly on his guard if he had ever suspected what she was doing. It was evident that he was always trying to emit the fact that everything was fine, and that his life held no problems for him. He was fighting a losing battle as almost everyone who knew him well, were aware of the great sadness in his life. She was delighted to find that as every day passed he was becoming more and more relaxed and that soon she might even be able to confront him and get him to 'open up', so that he might be able to cast out the demons which were causing him so much obvious distress. But, she was very patient and was very willing not to rush into anything that could frighten him away and make him close up forever.

Every day was like a wonderful live history lesson and the foursome were all very enthusiastic.

It had been noticed by everyone on the coach that the temperature in Quebec had fallen considerably since they had left New York, even before it had been pointed out by the courier, and even though the trip from Quebec to Montreal was only a mere 150 miles, they could all feel the temperature rising again as they motored south.

The trip had seemed to take no time at all compared with the 386 miles motored from Boston to Quebec, and no one on the coach had ever been aware before that the city of Montreal had been built on an island in the middle of the St. Lawrence River near Lake Ontario. It only measured 32 miles by 10 miles and that during the winter months it was so cold that they had even built an underground city so that the people would not have to venture outside, unless they really needed to. The city comprised of 2,000 shops, apartments and a cathedral and even a railway station.

Everyone gasped at the cleverness and the feat of engineering was awesome.

Again the city was grand and there was much to see, the shops again and the restaurants. In the evening they tripped out into the countryside to a quaint cabin type restaurant in the woods, which was very subtly lit with a very welcoming roaring fire in an open hearth and a very romantic atmosphere.

The day after was spent visiting a reconstruction of an old settlement, with primitive houses constructed from wood. The only means of water was drawn from a creek lower down the hill, which served all the community and invited diseases like typhoid, and other fever type illnesses, until many years later when improvements were made for better living.

Again, after another relatively, short journey of 120 miles they drove into the majestic Canadian Capital city of Ottawa. It was a city which sparkled with cleanliness and very few high rise buildings which was very refreshing, as all the skyscraper towers could become monotonous, if you allowed them to be, and could be very overpowering at times.

They were still in the Province of Ontario and after a quick shower and a change of clothing were taken on a trip around the city which included a tour around a native Indian museum and afterwards free time to explore. All that was eventually followed with another superb French meal in yet another authentic styled restaurant.

Both Joe and Maddie had indulged in a little more alcoholic sustenance that night which had removed many of their inhibitions. They felt even more comfortable with each other that night. As each day had passed they were relaxing more and more and tonight they were both sanguine.

Maddie looked awesome, resplendent in a simple black dress with a classical diamond pin scintillating in the light of the flickering flames. Joe looked at her in admiration of the entire woman and sighed at what might have been. Could have been.

....

They had all been very impressed with Ottowa. It was an exceptional city, but naturally they had to leave and be on their way again after only a single night's stay there. Nevertheless, after an extremely early start in the morning, during their journey from there, which would take them 225 miles to Toronto. Their courier found sufficient time to take them all on a sailing excursion around the 'Thousand Islands', which is a natural phenomena, with tiny islands, all dotted within a short distance from one another on the St. Lawrence River, many of them being occupied by settlers, usually as holiday residences. After a very pleasant few hours sailing around the pretty islands, they had continued on to Kingston, where they explored a prominent fortress, and eventually left the very imposing structure and at the same time leaving the mighty St. Lawrence river behind them, to go on to Lake Ontario, but not before they had called for some luscious apple pie which was a known and famous delicacy in that part of the country.

On arriving at their hotel they were all surprised to hear that they had just missed quite a significant earth tremor which had occurred at 4 o'clock, only three hours before and thanked providence because they, none of them, had any ambition to experience any such phenomena.

The first place to be visited that night was the C.N. Tower in Toronto, which was the highest domed tower, and the world's tallest freestanding structure. It had a glass enclosed elevator and glass floor. These structures had inflicted the eeriest of feelings on everyone, as one could imagine walking on air and feeling very insecure.

Catherine, true to form, preferred to stay on solid ground, Joe could not blame her. He secretly wished that he had volunteered to join her and never left the foyer, but decided to join the others hoping that his nerve would hold out. He did not regret it, but vowed that it would be the last time he would attempt to venture into nerve racking places, just for the sake of saying that he had been there!

Again, after the usual exploration of shopping malls, buying sprees and pioneer creek villages they were all shown a very ordinary looking street. It was actually the beginning of the famous Yeong Street which runs one thousand miles straight from Toronto to Manitoba. There they had the privilege of meeting an original American Indian. Not at all what anyone could have imagined. Not someone straight out of a John Wayne film but a smart and intelligent individual who entertained them all with interesting stories of past events and awe inspiring quotes, one of which left Joe with much food for thought, (quote) "The value of life, lies not in the length of days, but in the use that you make of them", unquote (Montaigne).

When their new acquaintance had left them, they all laughed, all being ashamed of their own infantile perceptions of modern day Native Indians. Joe had related how when he was a child his grandmother had told him that when she was a child the newspapers of the day were still reporting on battles between the natives and new settlers, and so, Joe and his friends were still united in the belief that all Indians were still all living on reservations given to them by the Central Government. Some actually were by choice still trying to live the 'old' way, but the majority had melted into the community like the immigrants who had settled there earlier.

…………………........

It was only a ninety mile run to Niagara from Toronto and not one person on the coach could have been disappointed at the first sight of the falls. The cascades were awesome. The scenery and parklands around the falls were also very pretty and most people wanted to either fly over the whole area in an helicopter, or sail to the mighty spectacle for a closer look on the 'Maid of the Mist', which was a boat,which sailed rather too close for comfort as far as a lot of the passengers were concerned.

Joe, again true to form decided to give both excursions a miss and enjoyed a lovely but solitary lunch in full view of both the American and the Canadian Horseshoe Falls without ever getting wet, leaving Maddie, as usual, participating in every way she could.

The party had only just booked into the hotel when a warning was issued via the television that a tornado was heading in their direction and would most likely hit Niagara and Lake Erie. Amazingly, no one seemed to panic, because everyone appeared to be stunned and then almost immediately the skies started to darken and a freak storm, presumably preceding the tornado, whisked up leaves and other debris before delivering and planting two inch hail stones which showered down unmercifully in every direction. Fortunately, and with a great relief to everyone, the storm passed as quickly as it had started, but it was quite an experience and thankfully it had happened after they had all left the falls.

That evening they had all been booked into the 'Skylon' for dinner, which was another scary experience for the faint hearted. They had all had to board an outside elevator which took only fifty eight seconds to place them in the rotating restaurant at the top of the very tall tower overlooking the mighty falls.

The view again was spectacular, the food and wine divine, and the piano music delightful. The only problem was coming down again! Joe was glad though that he had gone one final time up the great tower because the view of the falls from that angle could not be missed and would, like many other things, be remembered forever.

Back at the hotel Joe apologised to Maddie for his apparent cowardice. She smiled and excused him saying that she knew that was not the case and he could put it down to most likely having a phobia, which was not easy to overcome. But then she looked quiet and unresponsive and in deep thought most of the time. He was quite unnerved by this because Maddie had never, ever before shown any signs of moodiness or displeasure when she had been with him. If fact, she had always been the first to laugh and tease him about his nervousness before.

He carried on with small talk for quite some time but her attitude remained the same as she sat facing herself in the dressing table mirror. Appearing to be totally absorbed in her thoughts and unaware of him standing at the back of her and in full view. He then proceeded to make them coffee from the travelling kettle and toyed with the idea of leaving her alone for a while, but then made a decision to ask her what the matter was, and had he done something wrong, or said something to upset her?

It was no good letting the matter run along any further without trying to rectify it. He was very apprehensive about confronting her for fear of what she had to say would not be what he wanted to hear.

Joe said simply, "What's wrong Maddie?" but he was in for the shock of his life when she slowly turned and answered him.

…………………….......

"It's no good Joe. I have tried my best not to confront you in the past and I managed very well before we came here on this holiday, but being here with you constantly has altered things somewhat. I am going to have to level with you and be completely truthful because that is my way, and of course to be fair to you". She shrugged in a kind of hopeless way and paused. Joe was horrified, and the familiar feeling of foreboding began to creep over him. He had convinced himself that Maddie, seeing him continually, had discovered either faults or some kind of discrepancies in him that she could not tolerate. Being the straight, honest woman she was, she just had to tell him, leaving him under no illusions about their future relationship. He was wrong.

Maddie continued. Looking him straight in the face her eye contact never deviating. Her face was solemn and Joe thought he could detect moisture in her eyes. "I have got to call a spade a spade, as it were, there is no other way for me to do this. The fact is Joe, that I can no longer pretend and hide the fact of how very much I love you!"

Joe's heart thumped so loudly he could actually hear

the pulsing of it and the throbbing choked in his throat. He had anticipated the worst and was hearing the best and could not believe it.

Maddie gulped and then continued again. "You know Joe, I am fully aware of how disastrous your marriage has been and I have never really spoken to you about it in great detail as I felt that if you wished to say something about it, then you would. Even though I know that you are fond of me Joe, I have really never known how fond. Like a sister, a friend, or what? I just cannot wait any longer to find out, whatever your answer will be. I must know".

Her eyebrows raised now not humorously, as usual, but questioningly and asking for some kind of response from him.

Joe never looked away continuing the eye contact all the while and the only movement he made for some seconds was to shift his feet.

Maddie was the one now who was waiting in anticipation, watching his still stoic stance and felt sure that he was working out how to tell her that her feelings were not reciprocated. She was fearful of his reply should it be not what she was wanting to hear, but in actual fact had she known how shocked and astonished he was to hear her revelations, and that he was for some considerable time rendered speechless, which was agony for them both.

At last, after composing himself he was in control again, and his self confidence was reinstated. Now he could be true to himself. He had nothing at all to lose.

"Oh! Maddie. I have been so terrified of everything, including how I feel about you. I have been treading on egg shells trying not to let you know how I feel lest I should lose your friendship, because a serious relationship may not have been what you wanted at all. Being your friend is much better than not having you at all. So you see, we have both been secretive for the right reasons, but for far too long, and now, I suppose after learning the facts and having cleared the air I can honestly tell you that I feel exactly the same. I love you dearly Maddie, unconditionally, and would never want to be apart from you again. We have a lot to talk about I think and I can promise you that there will never be any more secrets".

Relief overwhelmed Maddie, so much so, that she felt light headed. "You don't have to be apart from me again Joe", she cried as she and Joe embraced each other with a wonderful tenderness that Joe had never known before. "We can work something out, I know we can". And Joe sighed with sheer joy enveloping him.

…………………….........

That night there was no climbing into separate beds, or falling straight asleep even though they were very tired, but they had felt invigorated by the unfolding confessions and laid cuddled up together entwined into the curves of their bodies, something that Joe had not done for so many years and never with his wife.

Joe had taken his first step over the rainbow, but could wait for the pot of gold. One step at a time. Nothing to rush frantically for. He had taken this holiday as 'Time Out' and it was certainly reaping its rewards.

Maddie started to ask questions once they were snuggled up. She started gently, but this time was not expecting any negative responses. She would try to eliminate his obvious skeletons one by one and eradicate them once and for all, as they were none of them illusory and then she would try to install some kind of equilibrium into his life, and not before time.

She adored him and caressed him and then she started. "Tell me. Tell me Joe then. Tell me everything. Leave nothing out. Start at the beginning and then I shall be able to understand perfectly the type of life that you have endured".

Joe responded quickly and directly and left nothing out. The bitter sweet life he had had and the empty future that he had felt was the only thing that he had to look forward to.

Like he had stated once before to her, the devil was in the detail and so everything that he felt and thought all tumbled out without any hesitation. Afterwards, he felt cleansed and whole, as though he had been into some glorious confessional and unloaded his very soul.

The emotional effort exerted by his verbal outpourings spent him physically and mentally making him extremely exhausted. It was only then that the pair of them equally exhausted, fell into a deep sleep encased in each others arms.

………………………........

Day ten of the tour, the ecstatic couple awoke to a beautiful sunny day and before they left Niagara to continue on their journey the tour operator took them all to Goat Island, which is a strip of land between the two great falls. All the travellers bent down and touched the crystal clear icy waters before the swirling torrent actually tumbled over the cataract. But because they had a long journey before them back into the United States, they could not linger very long but were thoroughly pleased to have had the privilege.

Their journey now took them through New York State, passing the town of Buffalo and on into Pennsylvania. Seeing the Susquehanna River which is 440 miles long, then all along the scenic route passing glorious villages built from timber, all painted bright colours and the tour only pausing for a luncheon break at a 'Farmhouse Cupboard' roadside restaurant before motoring on and finishing the 325 miles drive to Harrisburg, home to the Amish community, who are of Dutch descent and still manage to maintain the origins of their very strict ways of life.

During the next day a conducted tour was led around the countryside showing the way of life shared by the community. Time was spent looking around an authentic farm and house, showing everything to still be very primitive with absolutely nothing materialistic. The schools and all the countryside were all neat and tidy, but wherever they travelled there was no verbal response from the citizens, only on occasions a very polite nod. The outside world, to them was not welcome.

The tourists were surprised, delighted and amused by the names of the towns. There was Oxford and Cambridge to name but a few because, after all, as their courier said this was New England.

The four friends found a lovely cafe in a little mall in a place named 'Intercourse', which provided them with a divine lunch where they sat watching the passers by. Joe and Maddie smiled at one another like idiots whilst trying not to let the others notice their new found liaison.

After leaving Harrisburg, which was the capital of Pennsylvania and surprisingly not Philadelphia as everyone had mistakenly thought. To go on to their next desination they followed in their coach many lovely trails and even passed the Battlefield at Gettisburg, so famous during the American Civil war. Then on through Maryland, Baltimore, Virginia and past Camp David, the country retreat of the President, until they reached the magnificent capital City of the United States of America, Washington, District Columbia.

………………………........

The following two days were spent in the capital and their hotel, large and splendid, was situated straight opposite the notorious Watergate building.

The four friends were a little disappointed not to be having dinner on the cruiser on the lovely Potomac River, which unfortunately had to be cancelled at the last minute, but were well compensated by being taken for dinner to the Great Union station followed by another extremely wonderful tour of the city illuminated by night.

There did not appear to be anything they missed. Memorials such as the Washington, Jefferson, Roosevelt, Lincoln, and J.F. Kennedy. All dedicated to the great American men. The city so large and so beautiful and not a skyscraper in sight.

The following day was spent around the White House and the Capitol building. Opposite the President's White house was a park, where everyone took a foot tour of the great black marble memorial to the American soldiers' Vietnamese war dead. No one had a dry eye and Joe had to summon up all his courage to pay his own personal respects to the men who had ended their own young lives the same way as his beloved son, who was never very far from his mind.

For an hour or two Maddie and Joe spent a private period on their own on the steps of the Capitol Building feeding the numerous jet black squirrels and watching their comical antics. It felt as though they had both been like this forever, they were both as one. Contentment eradicating and easing any previous doubts. There were no more barriers between them, they were so relaxed and comfortable in each others company.

After that short respite they meandered back to the hotel passing the theatre where President Abraham Lincoln was shot and assassinated, then past the Federal Bureau of Investigation to pick up the coach again. An excursion to the Arlington cemetery followed, to see the thousands of graves of fallen heroes and the graves of the Kennedy family, which, when they arrived surprised everyone by being so bland and unassuming.

All the residents of the cemetery had died violently and Joe grieved for the futility of it all.

The rest of that day was spent resting as the following day would be very tiring. Joe and Maddie lay quietly on their beds, reflecting on the holiday and flowing into deep discussion on every other issue.

After a short silence Maddie started. "Joe, why do you think that Trudie would have preferred not to be married at all?"

Joe's eyes squinted as he raised his head to look at her. The question had come as a surprise. "How do you mean? I don't know. Just not the marrying kind, I suppose. She's a man hater".

Another pause from Maddie as she hesitated before she continued. "You really don't know, do you Joe?"

"Know. Know what?", he sounded puzzled by the statement.

Maddie was faltering and Joe was quizzing her now.

"Come on Maddie, don't be shy. If you have something to say, then say it. Remember, no more secrets. It can't be any worse than any of the things I have told you".

"Alright. It's about her sexuality, and due to her archaic upbringing. Her sexual leanings would have been prohibited in those days. Have you ever considered that or

174

discussed it with her?"

"Are you trying to tell me something that I was never aware of? Are you saying what I think you are saying? And if you are, how long have you known?"

"Ever since I was at school with her". Maddie said without hesitation, "but when she became pregnant and married you we all thought that she had either gone straight or was bi-sexual". Maddie then shrugged with half a sympathetic smile which said 'you poor naive, trusting man, what a fool you have been' but nothing was put into words. Actions were clearer in this case.

Now Joe fully understood and he felt free and exonerated. He no longer had the heaviness of feeling that he had in some way been responsible for all the heartache over the years. He felt like a man again instead of some frail shadow of one. The truth had been said, and he loved Maddie all the more for it, far more than he could ever express.

The next day they were up with the larks again and on to Philadelphia where they all enjoyed a tasty lunch in a local bistro but after a short drive around the city and the touching of the famous Liberty Bell, they all reluctantly alighted the coach for their final journey of the tour to the J.F.Kennedy airport in New York for their long flight back to England and home.

Chapter Ten

During the long flight back to the U.K., Joe could not really discuss any of the issues previously talked about with Maddie whilst they were away on holiday, due to the lack of privacy on the aircraft, but he had had much time to think and recapitulate on many of their deliberations.

He smiled when he remembered how very nervous he had been originally, when Maddie had asked him in her forthright manner, why he had not left Trudie before this time.

He remembered that he had paused for a short time to ferret through his grey celled computer and once again he had inevitably failed to find a realistic and positive answer. His only explanation had been a combination of what seemed to present themselves as pitiful excuses.

Still smiling he remembered fondly that the only time that he could recollect Maddie scolding him was only in exasperation saying, "I am no sage, not really so wise Joe, but I must say that I do not care about what you are willing to forget, but what you are willing to remember. Show some mettle lad!" She had ranted quietly with an element of some aside but still only really pretending to be cross. "Try to be more macho", she had paused and with raised eyebrows had pointed a wagging finger in pretence of his being scolded and warned "But. Only with her! Be as smooth an operator as she is".

He now fully realised that he had been hiding behind a

facade, showing one face to the world and another in private, hoping that no one would ever notice. In truth that was a fallacy as everyone was aware of the unhappiness that Joe had tolerated and indeed, was still doing, but now only to a certain extent. Things were about to change.

He could accept and welcome the constructive criticism from Maddie. He could now admit to himself that he had been too submissive and not assertive enough from the start.

He had listened intently to her words of wisdom, when she had pointed out that before he was totally destroyed he now had a choice. Everything about his future was now possible to arrange. This relationship with Maddie was no clandestine affair, he knew that it wasn't. He knew beyond any doubt that Maddie was the woman he wanted to spend the rest of his life with. She was his soul mate. The world could be their oyster, she would be willing to travel with him to see all his friends and he would be happy to accommodate her in anything that she would wish to do.

He looked over at her now, the love in his eyes reaching out and she turned and beamed knowing full well what he was thinking and nodded in her acknowledgement.

If the happy couple were under any illusion that the rest of the tour passengers were oblivious of their romantic alliance they were wrong. Much chattering had been obvious as all the passengers were all delighted and elated in unison at their new found friends loving liaison.

The happiest of them all were Jack and Catherine Hillam. They were ecstatic. It had proved to be a wonderful conclusion to a perfect holiday and had resulted in working out just as they had prophesied and hoped would come to fruition, even before they had all embarked on the holiday.

……………………........

The touchdown at Heathrow Airport was smooth and the weather sunny even though there was a slight nip in the air. Joe inhaled the sweet air and felt like a new man as they were all ushered to their Internal flights terminal for their short flight back into Manchester airport.

Tearful goodbyes were said and addresses exchanged to the other passengers who were all taking off in different directions. A kind of sadness enveloped everyone as they had all become quite close living and touring in such close proximity for almost three weeks, and to perhaps never see one another ever again. They had all shared a special camaraderie and much joy and laughter and would be sadly missed for quite some time. Manchester airport was reached in just short of one hours flight and after passing through passport control, then through baggage collection the taxi cab driver ordered previously was waiting for them as they came through the arrival lounge. Just over one hour later the four friends were situated in their respective houses.

Joe was dropped off the last at his own request. No need to make any waves at this point in time. He wanted everything to flow smoothly….. he had had enough of trouble and had a strategic plan worked out in his head.

The house door was locked. He reached for his key and placed it into the lock. The lock had been changed. He knocked hard on the door and after a few seconds of humiliation at having to stand on his own doorstep the door opened.

Trudie stood there, hostile as ever, showing an arrogance proving her disease of spirit as her eyes narrowed before she silently stepped aside allowing him through into the hallway.

He placed his cases at the foot of the staircase and with equal silence made his way to the kitchen in order to boil a kettle of water for a long awaited cup of tea.

She followed and then she spoke. "I have been decorating the bedrooms since you went away", she said without any emotion at all.

Joe turned to face her but did not speak.

"When you take your bags upstairs, put them in the second bedroom. I have bought two double beds. One for each bedroom. We may as well start as we mean to go on. Living separate lives, I mean". Now she was showing some trace of triumph in her embittered facial expression.

Joe looked at her but still did not answer, his own expression showing only revulsion and despising which was completely alien to his previous make up. He brewed the tea and filled his cup and then silently turned and climbed the stairs leaving the luggage still where he had left it when he had initially walked in.

He entered into the master bedroom which was painted all white and looked stark with only the duvet cover to break the whiteness. He then meandered into the second bedroom which again was painted all white, with nothing at all to break the monotony. He sat on the bed looking around the room. No pictures or mirrors on the walls. No ornaments, the room was inanimate. A feeling of déjà vu overwhelmed him. He knew previously that his decision to leave was already made but if he had had doubts he would now have known immediately that his decision was positively made.

His estranged wife was treating him like some kind of pariah. He knew beyond any doubt that she would be downstairs revelling, and enjoying every moment of imagining that she was upsetting him again, only this time the tables had turned and it was he who would be calling the tune. Against his usual nature, he knew that this time he would be the one relishing the situation.

There was nothing remiss about his decision, there was no way at all that he should feel obligated to her. Any other person would most likely have left her many years ago.

She had played straight into his hands and he could not have manufactured the situation any better had he tried. She was totally unaware of what was to come.

Joe arose from the bed and opened the wardrobe door. He took out a large holdall and then quickly emptied all the drawers, putting the remainder of his clothes into the bag. A photograph album containing pictures of his parents and David was carefully packed into the bottom of the bag. His collection of books, which had previously been lovingly housed in a bookcase, were now unceremoniously packed in cardboard boxes and stood on the floor.

Joe was disgusted at her contempt of him, but at least now he could bear anything.

He turned and carried the bag and the boxes downstairs in turn and opened the outside door. One by one he loaded his possessions into his car and then reversed it out of the garage and onto the drive.

He then returned into the house and went upstairs again and looked around the room and winced at the thought that after all these years, these were his only precious possessions. He wanted nothing else. The other things in the house had all been touched by her.

Joe then meandered again slowly down the stairs and found Trudie still in the kitchen. He knew that she would have been fully aware of his actions since arriving home but would have been too 'pig-headed', to even ask him what he was doing, even though she would have been more than eager to know. She would not have given Joe the satisfaction of asking him.

She turned to face him as he entered the room with a

smirk on her face that said it all, but that expression was quickly wiped away when she realised that Joe did not appear to be in the least perturbed by her vile actions.

"I'm going". Joe said simply but flatly.

"Going?" Trudie repeated, her voice faltering and reflecting her obvious and absolute surprise. "Going where?"

"Where I am going is of no concern to you. All you need to know, before you put on the usual act of panicking, is that I never ever had anything from you and I want nothing from you now. You can live in your bland, sterile, and unwelcoming house for the rest of your life, but not with me. You can do just what you want. Live with or without your girlfriends. Take in a partner, if you wish. But Heaven help her if you do. You know, the ones you always thought I knew nothing about!" Joe said triumphantly, pleased that now he had some ammunition to fire and keeping up the pretence that he had known about her secret all along.

Joe continued, keeping up the barrage of words he had kept contained within for so very many years. "I want nothing more to do with you at all. All I shall take are my tools and my car. The rest, as they say, my dear, are yours. Do not try to contact me personally. Should you find out where I am, do not contact me. If you need to ask me anything at all then you can contact my Solicitor, he will deal with you from now on. The divorce papers will be served within the next few days." Joe was the one who stood in cold silence now, anticipating feeling some measure of pleasure, which would have been alien to him before, but he was mistaken for he felt no triumph at all just a feeling of overwhelming release.

Trudie looked as though she had been poleaxed now that the full realisation of Joe actually knowing about her secretive life finally dawned upon her, but after a few seconds which she obviously took to compose herself she started to be effusive, her gushing manner only resulting in utter disgust showing plainly on Joe's face and her being aghast at recognising that look never before seen on her mild mannered husband's face. She was not deterred and she continued, almost to plead, asking him to reconsider his intentions and pointed out what he had to lose by not staying there. They could still pursue their own lives as they had always done in the past. What had changed?

Joe was not about to justify his actions or decisions to her. She had absolutely no rights after the way she had never had any reservations about manipulating him in the past to achieve her own ends. Even now he was not seeking retribution, but only a life to be rid of her, never to even think about her again. He thought once again about the wise Native American Indian and his recited adages, which had impressed him so very much, 'Yesterday's History, Tomorrow's a mystery and Today is a gift'. Now was the time to live before the grim reaper intervenes and strikes again. Live and celebrate every day as it comes and with that thought he picked up the rest of his belongings and closed the door behind him. He never looked back.

……………………........

Joe's car seemed to drive itself to his father's house, but by this time it was quite late and everywhere was in darkness. He knew that Bob would be now well and truly ensconced in Cissy's house, in the nicest possible way, and they would have been sound asleep for quite some time and so he was not about to rouse them.

There would be plenty of time and much to say to them

in the morning.

He felt quite exhilarated again at the thought, because he knew that the pair of them would be very pleased and excited about the news and the significant result.

He made no noise at all as he turned the key in the door of his old home. He looked around and everything, as always felt so very comfortable. He was very weary now, it had been a very tiring day, all the travelling, the excitement, the decisions and the outcome of his confrontation with Trudie. No matter how confident he had assured himself that he was, it was still undertaken with an element of trepidation. Fortunately, it had finally given him a new confidence and resulted in an assertiveness he never thought he had possessed. But it was all over now.

Surprisingly the water was piping hot, as if his father had known all the while, where Joe would be spending his first night home. He thankfully climbed into the bath and soaked until the water was almost cold and then he towelled himself dry and dropped naked and exhausted into bed, totally spent. After trawling the sheets for a cool place to lay his hot feet and promising himself that he would take Trevor Watson quietly aside at some time in the near future and ever so gently inform him about his wonderful biological son, whom Joe himself had had the real pleasure of knowing and bringing up. He was still in deep thought when he fell into an utterly contented sleep.

…………………….......

Joe awoke with the sun streaming into the bedroom and the smell of bacon sizzling and the aroma of steaming coffee winding its way up the staircase. It reminded him of the morning after his mother had died, when they were all

183

so grief stricken, but now was a time for rejoicing and he felt that he could feel his mother's presence and happily felt that she would be celebrating with them. It gave him a positive feeling of comfort.

He quickly arose and threw on a robe and without even his face being washed pelted down the stairs.

There they both stood in the kitchen. His father and Cissie, both turning as he entered the room, smiles of anticipation spanning all over their faces. They did not really need to be told that he had left Trudie, they could read him like a book. After hugs and kisses they were itching to be told every detail. Everything that had transpired since he last said his goodbyes before his holiday.

Joe decided to tease them and motioned that he would have to have a shower and dress before breakfast but that he would not be very long! They shrugged with feigned exasperation as he disappeared again upstairs.

The breakfast had been luscious and had gone straight to the spot, after his third cup of the filtered coffee he comically decided to put them out of their misery. He started to relate in full detail the whole of his holiday, his wonderfully, fabulous relationship with Maddie and of course the significant outcome and result of his victorious homecoming.

Both Bob and Cissie could be forgiven for showing an element of pomposity, when they were listening to Joe's account of his final showdown with Trudie, which showed on both their faces, but only because they were so joyous about his new found freedom, so well deserved and so long in coming.

When breakfast was over and the table cleared, Cissie discreetly motioned that she had chores to do in her own house and thoughtfully left Bob and Joe to have some prime time together where they could easily indulge in private talk that Joe would have perhaps not have wanted to reiterate upon unless he could speak to his father alone. She was right.

The men had sat silently for a short while, almost reflecting on the time when Joe's mother, Celia, had been so tragically killed, although now it was a happy time, not a time to be contemplating sorrow. A time to look forward to much better times and the thought refreshed Bob. Now he realised that Joe would be enjoying his life after he had gone and this thought sated him beyond anything he could ever have dreamed of before.

"Shall we have a day fishing dad?" Joe suggested "We could have plenty of thinking time and precious time together, it is a beautiful day".

"That's alright by me. Long time since I went angling. It will do us both the world of good", Bob answered quickly, wishing to grant as many wishes to his precious son as he possibly could. He had always tried to be there for him, through thick and thin times but unfortunately, he always felt that there was a shadow crowding him about not telling Joe in the early days about what he and Celia had believed about Trudie. He knew that Joe would never hold that misdemeanour against him, but he found it very difficult to forgive himself. They could have avoided all the heartache and averted all the pain. No matter, he could not backtrack and rectify anything, just go forward and hope upon hope that all would go well from now on in.

………………….........

By the time both men returned back home from their fishing trip, Joe had made his final decision.

The final night of the holiday had been spent with

Maddie and he discussing in great depth where their relationship was going when they returned home. It had been decided at that time that there was no immediate rush to make rash decisions that could be regretted afterwards. It was suggested that whatever conclusion Joe came to would be absolutely fine with Maddie, which was so thoughtful and gracious, but which wholly mirrored her nature.

If he decided to take her up on her generous offer, her house would be his house. His home. Her daughter and son in law would be delighted that her mother had found a lovely companion and especially that now they were expecting their first child. Maddie was so excited at the prospect of becoming a grandmother giving Joe a chance at being a step grandfather the world could be rosy for them all.

Alternatively, if he decided either to stay with Trudie or live in his parents' house, then there would be no hard feelings. Joe knew that life was too short to throw away lifelines and the thought of perhaps having Trudie entering his mind again made him shudder.

After dinner of fresh river trout, cooked slowly in brown butter and eaten with great gusto by the three of them, Joe decided to have an early night. He had not so far contacted Maddie in any way as he had promised not to do so until his mind was inextricably made up, absolutely and irrevocably one way or the other so as not to confuse or give her any false hope and be cruelly let down later, should he change his mind. He would not, nor could not, have done that to her and would never have taken advantage of her loving nature.

He knew that she was the one that he wanted to be with for all time, but he did not want her to think that he was being presumptuous or too eager at making up his mind without mulling everything over first. But, he could not wait for the morning.

He rose with the larks the following day and quickly showered. He pulled on a pair of slacks and a silk shirt and picked up his watch throwing his gold wedding ring into the waste paper basket at his feet. His clothes had been freshly laundered by Cissie the day before whilst he and his father were fishing and so he quickly packed everything, scrawled out a note for when they awoke, telling his hosts where he would be and thanking them for their humility. With a nimbleness and quickness he had forgotten he had, he pulled his shoulders back, sped down the stairs and into the car.

…………………........

When he drew into the drive of Maddie's house, his heart was thumping with ultimate excitement, but he could not in all honesty remember driving the journey between his father's house and Maddie's. It was as though he was robotic again or someone else had driven him there.

He slowly drew to a halt and applied the brakes of the car, alighted, and then locked the doors. He could feel that his heart was still turning somersaults until it almost choked him, the excitement welling up in anticipation of what was to come was paramount in his thoughts up until it was almost impossible to contain any longer.

He traced his way up the front path until he was facing the huge oak front door when he gently pressed the bell and waited, rooted to the spot like some frightened child.

The door opened slowly and Maddie stood there in her robe, radiant, exuding a rosy glow after recently bathing. She said nothing. He said nothing. They both knew why he was there and the look of love emitting from their eyes in perfect harmony left nothing to doubt.

Maddie lifted both his hands and placed them evenly on either of her cheeks, caressing each hand with her soft skin and then she brought them down and kissed them separately.

He in turn then cupped her lovely face in his hands and brought her lips towards him where he kissed them softly, gently, time after time. Not with hot passion, just a deep and loving tenderness and a sincere feeling of precious love and belonging.

Still nothing was said as she quietly and slowly drew him into the house and closed the door.

Joe John Bullimore was home at last....